ARRIVAL

ARRIVAL

THE PALADINS—BOOK ONE

RICHARD LEE BYERS

Charlotte, NC

FALSTAFF
BOOKS

WWW.FALSTAFFBOOKS.COM

For Doug Blythe

William stood waiting in the darkness. Even in the coolness that had descended on Acre with the coming of night, the multiple layers of cloth and mail he wore, the garb and armor that marked him as a Knight Templar, felt uncomfortable. Or perhaps it was the business at hand that was truly wearing on him.

"What are we doing here?" he whispered, too softly for Pierangelo, the commander of this nocturnal expedition, to overhear.

"What we're told," Gaspard whispered back. Lanky, with a crooked and close-lipped smile, he stood midway in both age and rank between William and Pierangelo, and unlike either, had been born here in Outremer. "Be quiet and keep watching."

William sighed and did as he was bidden, even though the task was likely pointless. A high-ranking Knight of the Hospital, a counterpart to Pierangelo or someone even more senior, would surely ride out of his order's stronghold through the main gate. He wouldn't sneak out this little postern around the back. If *anyone* came out—and as the hours passed, that seemed increasingly unlikely—it would almost certainly be a low-ranking Hospitaler going to visit a woman. William hadn't been in Acre a week before discovering, to his dismay, that knights of his order sometimes flouted their own rule of celibacy in similar fashion. Indeed, he suspected Gaspard was one such knight, although that hadn't kept him from liking the veteran who was more willing than most to teach a newcomer how to get along.

But eventually, to William's surprise, the little gate *did* open, and three men slipped out. In the shadows, they were ghostly and anonymous in nondescript hooded cloaks. William and his companions might almost have been looking at themselves.

The men from the Hospital set off down a crooked and all but lightless street, a street that, at this hour, was empty except for themselves. The Templars gave them a head start, then followed. William tried to move as Gaspard had instructed him, silently and carefully to keep the trio ahead from noticing they were being shadowed.

Despite his misgivings, the youngest Templar took some satisfaction in competently performing as he was supposed to, but then realized that the very leader who had laid out the goal of the surveillance was now jeopardizing it. Gradually, as though unable to restrain himself, Pierangelo quickened his stride and narrowed the distance between him and the men ahead. Short-haired but bearded like all Templars, he had a scarred brow, fierce gray eyes, and a perpetual scowl that intimidated William and made him resemble some implacable warrior saint.

William and Gaspard exchanged glances and kept pace with their leader. As they walked faster, they perforce became less stealthy, and their mail rattled and clinked. The sounds were small, soft, but inwardly, William winced at each of them until the moment came when a noise carried across the dwindling divide and the three men from the Hospital spun around.

The one in the middle caught William's particular attention by taking a step backward and putting his companions between the Templars and himself. It was only what many a lord or other person in authority would have done, looking to his underlings to protect him, but Pierangelo did nothing comparable. In any confrontation, he was always in the forefront.

The Hospitaler leader was a sandy-haired man with a square, handsome face. He wasn't truly fat, but looked well fed in a way that Templars, whose Rule included stipulations as to what they could eat and drink, seldom did. He pushed back the wings of his mantle, which exposed the black surcoat with the white cross blazon beneath and gave him easy access to his sword. The Hospitaler on his left, Pierangelo, and Gaspard all did the same, the Templars thus revealing their white surcoats with red cross emblems. After a moment's hesitation, William followed suit, while praying no one would actually be reckless enough to reach for a blade.

"Sir Pierangelo," the Hospitaler leader said.

"Sir Ottomar," Pierangelo replied.

"When I heard footsteps," Ottomar said, "I suspected thieves were stalking us. How welcome to see that in fact, you're fellow soldiers of Christ."

"Where are you going?" Pierangelo asked.

"We're just patrolling the city," Ottomar said. "Making sure all's well." He shrugged. "Sleep eludes me sometimes."

Pierangelo sneered. "It's been years since you deigned to undertake any duty that a true man-at-arms might perform. Who are you sneaking out to see? What are you plotting?"

After he had arrived from England, one of the first and greatest astonishments that had overtaken William was the discovery of the bitter political divisions in the Christian lands on the southern shores of the Mediterranean. Perhaps he would have had a better notion of the true nature of affairs had his family back in Devon played a more prominent role in matters of state. But they were just obscure rustic gentry, leaving a younger son to imagine that Templars, Hospitalers, and all the other Crusaders were faithful comrades fighting as one to complete the liberation of the Holy Land.

The real situation was nothing like that. The Crusader lords were squabbling for precedence, wealth, and to advance the interests of patrons across the sea like the King of France and Emperor Frederick. Each had formed alliances with Muslim states that had their own complicated quarrels and rivalries. Even the Temple and the Hospital, formidable political players in their own right, had such ties, the former with Damascus and the latter with Cairo.

The newly arrived Richard, Earl of Cornwall, was supposed to find equitable resolutions to all disputes and bring unity to the Kingdom of Jerusalem. To that end, he had ordered that the various parties cease secretly conspiring with one another and that Templars and Hospitalers stop brawling in the streets of Acre.

So far, a grudging truce had held. Surely, William thought, it would hold now. Seasoned men like Pierangelo and Ottomar might feel the same rancor as their subordinates, but they would have the discipline not to act on it.

"I told you," Ottomar said, "we're simply checking for signs of trouble. And that's all I'm going to tell you. I don't answer to the Temple."

Pierangelo snorted. "If your intentions are innocent, you won't mind if my companions and I patrol along with you. If we come across any trouble, six will contend with it better than three."

Ottomar looked Pierangelo in the eye in a way that made it clear that, however he'd occupied himself in recent years, he too was a knight with a knight's martial training and experience of battle. "If I must be frank, your mistrust and lack of civility make your company unwelcome. I remind you again, you have no authority over us. Turn around and walk away."

"You presume to give me orders?" Pierangelo replied. "*Me?* A *true* servant of God?" He drew his sword and started forward. Gaspard murmured an obscenity and did the same.

William hesitated. This shouldn't be happening. He should stop it somehow. But even if he knew how, there was no time. The Hospitalers were already snatching their blades from their scabbards and assuming fighting stances, and it was inconceivable that he would abandon his brother knights to battle them alone. He too drew, advanced, and found himself facing the man who hadn't opened his cloak before.

Wiry with a pointed black beard and bushy brows, the fellow was ready to fight now, though, and the weapon in his hand was a curved scimitar, not the straight sword one would expect a Hospitaler to wield. He wasn't wearing the dark surcoat of the order, either. William faltered in surprise, and it nearly cost him when the scimitar flashed at his head. Trained reflex called forth a parry, though, he riposted with a slash to the belly, and his opponent saved himself by hopping a finger length out of range.

The next few exchanges confirmed William's initial impression. His adversary, whoever he was, was a skilled swordsman, nimble and smooth, limited only, perhaps, by overreliance on a couple of favorite combinations he tried repeatedly.

William wished he had his shield. He could defend with a blade alone if necessary, but he had more training fighting the other way. But wishing wouldn't help him win. He put it out of his mind to focus on the task at hand.

Despite his concentration, though, he caught glimpses of the other combatants as he and his opponent circled. Gaspard had engaged Ottomar's remaining companion. The Templar appeared to be the abler swordsman but had yet to press his advantage to land a killing stroke. With his face twisted in hatred, Pierangelo had found his way to Ottomar, either because he'd bypassed the Hospitaler leader's underlings or because, when violence erupted, Ottomar had after all come willingly to duel. The Templar leader was driving in hard. His expression intense but unafraid, Ottomar gave ground before him, concentrated on avoiding the relentless cuts, and, in all likelihood, waited for Pierangelo to make a mistake and open himself up.

A soprano voice started softly crooning. William didn't recognize the language but caught rhymes and cadence. The recitation was a poem, plainsong, or something similar. He wondered how he was able to hear it clearly over the clash of steel, the grunts of effort and rasp of labored breathing. He wondered where it was coming from but knew better than to take his eyes off his adversary to look for the source.

The scimitar made a short, probing cut. He beat the curved sword with his own and loosened his foe's grasp on the hilt. In the instant it took for the other man to tighten his fingers again, he stepped, slashed, and *nearly* scored, but alas, his adversary dodged just in time.

The recitation waxed louder until, if William hadn't known better, he would have believed the woman was chanting right behind him. It was strange, but he didn't let it distract him. He'd nearly defeated his opponent when he beat his blade. Now that he'd taken his measure, he was eager to finish the job.

His foe stepped in, feinted to the head, and cut to the

knee. It was one of his favorite combinations, one of the attacks William had learned to expect, and he swung his sword down to parry. But his blade didn't find the other because the other man had made a *double* feint. The true attack was flashing in high, and William couldn't bring his sword up in time to block it.

William threw himself backward and avoided the cut by a hair. But the frantic evasion tipped him off balance, and his back foot caught on an uneven spot in the cobblestones. He slammed down on his back, and his adversary rushed in to take advantage of his floundering vulnerability.

At the same moment, the woman, wherever she was, recited a phrase with particular emphasis and then fell silent. A chill and a dazzling brightness ran through the air together, as if William were back outside his family's modest excuse for a castle and looking out over the snow on a cold but sunny winter day.

Then he felt himself falling, even though that was impossible when he was already on his back. The sensation only lasted for a second, and then, if he'd truly taken a second fall, he landed so softly that he didn't feel an impact.

The man with the scimitar stopped short of making an attack. Instead, he stepped back and looked around.

Though William felt dazed and bewildered, instinct prompted him to stand up. He started to do so, and the movement whipped his foe's attention back to him. The other man raised his scimitar to threaten the Templar anew.

William went ahead and drew himself to his feet but did so very slowly. He pointed his own sword downward and raised his off hand to signal that he too wanted a cessation of hostilities. The man with the scimitar gave a nod, and then they both cast about.

The chill and the brightness had only lasted a heartbeat. The temperature was comfortable now, and the scene as dark as the street had been. They *weren't* in the street anymore, though. William could make out walls and pillars rising up and up to a vaulted ceiling; it was as if he and his companions had entered a cathedral. Windows placed well above the floor revealed slices of black sky and the stars shining therein, but he would have seen even less than he did if not for an orange light source—a lantern, possibly— glowing here inside the building.

The clash of steel cut through his numbed astonishment, and he jerked around. Gaspard and his opponent had ceased fighting, too, but Pierangelo and Ottomar hadn't. Obviously, that was the choice of the former and not the latter. The Hospitaler was saying, "Stop! Stop!" to no avail.

Gaspard sheathed his sword, rushed toward the two combatants, and, as he moved, maneuvered to come at Pierangelo from behind. William gleaned his intentions, and they were clearly wrong. A proper Templar was obedient. He wouldn't act to thwart a superior's will.

But in these bizarre circumstances, *not* intervening felt like it would be even more wrong. William hurried after Gaspard.

Gaspard grabbed Pierangelo by the sword arm. "Ottomar's right!" he said. "You should stop!"

"Let go!" Pierangelo struggled to wrench himself free and nearly succeeded before William seized him by the other arm.

"Please, sir!" William said. "This isn't the time! Look around!"

Pierangelo strained to break loose for another moment. Then, perhaps recognizing the futility of his efforts, he yielded to his subordinates' entreaties and surveyed his surroundings. He stiffened in shock.

"Truce?" Ottomar said.

Twisting his head, Pierangelo gave each of his underlings a glare. "Unhand me."

This time Gaspard obeyed, so, hoping his friend hadn't misread Pierangelo's intentions, William did the same.

Pierangelo hitched his shoulders as if shaking off the lingering contamination of the junior Templars' insolence. "What's happened to us?" he demanded.

"I don't know," Ottomar replied, "but perhaps she can tell us." He nodded to his left.

William turned to see he'd been correct about the orange light. It was a lantern, and a woman had picked it up and was carrying it closer.

———————————

2

The light revealed the woman was tall and thin with long pale hair dangling over her shoulders in braids. William judged her to be around Gaspard's age. She was dressed like a man in a tunic, trousers, and boots seemingly made for rough outdoor wear, and even beyond the mismatch with her sex, there was something odd, unfamiliar about the cut of her attire. No expert on clothing, William just wasn't sure what the difference was. She had a long knife sheathed on one hip, a mace hanging from her belt on the other, and a book tucked under the arm not occupied with the lantern.

Her high forehead and long, narrow nose made her look intelligent, perhaps even scholarly, but her expression wasn't scholarly at the moment. She beamed at William and the others like a little girl beholding something wonderful.

It made him want to smile back, and he felt a pang of disappointment when her face changed an instant later. Now she looked uncertain, conceivably because she registered the ill will and suspicion still festering among the men that was now being directed at her.

A smile returned to her face, perhaps because she made an effort to put it there, and she spoke. It was the same soprano voice William had heard during the street fight, and it was employing the same unknown language as before.

Ottomar looked to the man with the scimitar, who shook his head to indicate that he didn't understand, either.

"Enough of this babble," Pierangelo said. He started forward.

Not presuming to lay hands on his commander again but hovering close enough that he *could* do so, Gaspard said, "She's done nothing wrong."

Speaking almost simultaneously, so their words overlapped, Ottomar said, "We may need her to give us answers."

"Then let's beat them out of her," Pierangelo replied. Still, perhaps perceiving that no one else was convinced that was the proper course of action, he stopped advancing.

The woman raised her hand as much as William had raised his to show he wanted to stop fighting. She then sat down on the floor, put the lantern in front of her, and positioned the book—it looked old, with a rotting blue leather cover, silver hinges tarnished black, and yellowed parchment leaves coming loose from the binding—to make best use of the light. She carefully turned the pages until she found the one she wanted, then started reading a rhyming, metered selection like the recitation in the street.

"Witch!" Pierangelo said. He reached for his sword.

"We don't know that," Gaspard said.

"Can't you tell she's casting a spell? Has she corrupted your mind already?'

Gaspard looked to Ottomar. "Sir, it's still as you said. We need the answers she can give us."

The Hospitaler leader didn't reply. For once he looked uncertain, caught between the hope that the woman could help them and the fear she meant to do something hideous, unable to decide even though there was no time to deliberate.

William was similarly unsure. The woman looked strange, her clothing perhaps indecent. Without a doubt, uncanny things were happening, and it certainly looked as if she might be responsible. If she was a witch, and they stood idle while she chanted her way through another incantation, there was no telling how dire the results might be.

Yet he just didn't feel like she meant them any harm. That initial joyful smile made nonsense of the whole idea.

William's erstwhile opponent raised his scimitar. Without knowing he meant to act until he did, William interposed himself between the man and the woman.

"Stand aside!" Pierangelo said.

William didn't know what he was going to do in response to that, either. Before his legs had a chance to show him, Gaspard said, "Look."

William risked a glance backward. The woman was now sprawled on her side. Apparently she'd fainted.

"Is everyone well?" Gaspard asked. "Nobody turned into a toad or anything like that?" Evidently no one had been, and he snorted. "I told you it would be all right."

"No thanks to you and Sir William," Pierangelo gritted, and inwardly, William flinched.

"What's wrong with her?" Ottomar asked.

Gaspard knelt beside the unconscious woman, held his hand in front of her nose and mouth, felt her forehead, and pressed his fingertips against the artery in the side of her neck. "She's alive. She doesn't have a fever. It's as if she simply stood up too fast and became lightheaded."

The Hospitaler Gaspard had fought spoke up. He had broad, round shoulders, a barrel chest, and bandy legs, and the scars of a pox he had at some point survived dotted his cheeks. "She didn't try to stand up."

Gaspard smiled his crooked smile. "I know. I said it was *like* that."

"Can you wake her?" Ottomar asked.

"I'm no physician, but I'll try." Patting the woman's cheeks, Gaspard said, "Wake up. Wake up." When that didn't work, he took a bit of the skin on her cheek between thumb and forefinger and pinched. She still didn't stir. "No luck. Apparently she'll have to wake in her own time."

"The Lord is merciful," Pierangelo said. "He's given us a chance to kill her without risk to ourselves."

"With all respect, sir," Gaspard said, "that's still not a wise idea for the same reasons as before."

"Fine," the senior Templar growled. "But we can at least disarm her, tie her up, gag her, and separate her from her book of curses."

The pox-scarred Hospitaler frowned. "No rope."

Gaspard took off his shabby cloak, cut it with a dagger to start a tear, then ripped away a strip of cloth. "This will do."

When the woman was bound, Ottomar said, "And now, introductions, I think. We might as well know what to call one another."

The pox-scarred Hospitaler said, "I'm Hauke, but everyone calls me Ox because I'm strong."

The man with the scimitar hesitated before giving his name and then said, "Jibril."

"A Saracen," Pierangelo said. "Who are you, *exactly*? Why were you sneaking around with two Knights of the Hospital in the dead of night?"

"That's our affair and none of yours," Ottomar said. "It's also irrelevant at the moment. Our immediate concern should be understanding our situation."

"Which is suddenly finding ourselves in a strange place," Gaspard said. "At the moment, we can't question our prisoner as to the why and the how, but perhaps if we step outside and look around, we can at least get our bearings."

"Agreed," Pierangelo said, albeit with a scowl that showed he wasn't yet willing to forgive Gaspard for what he regarded as his underling's insubordination. "But someone must stand guard over the witch, and it can't be the Saracen. I don't trust him."

"Then Ox will do it," Ottomar said.

Eyes narrowed, Pierangelo weighted the suggestion. Perhaps he didn't trust a Hospitaler much more than he trusted a Saracen, but he might also be considering that if he left one of his own men behind to stand guard, it would be a pair of Hospitalers plus an ally and only two Templars venturing out into the night.

Meanwhile, William felt an unaccustomed impatience. Loyal though he was to Pierangelo, it seemed to him that Ottomar had a point. For the time being, the divisions between the Temple and the Hospital no longer mattered.

"All right," Pierangelo said at length. "Your man bides here, and the rest of us will take a look around."

From their current location, they could just make out a black rectangle that was a doorway, open to the night as the windows overhead were. As William and his fellow scouts walked toward it, the orange lantern light fading with every step, Gaspard came up beside him and murmured, "Go quietly, like when we were following our new friends through the streets. We don't know what's waiting outside."

Indeed they didn't, but as they slipped out of the building, William was hoping for an indication that, though some mysterious agency had shifted them from one location to another, at least they were still in Acre. His first look around, however, provided no support for such optimism.

With only starlight to illuminate the scene, he still couldn't see particularly well, but his initial impression was one of ruin, buildings with roofs that had fallen in, columns toppled or broken short. Worse still, while he was no more a builder than he was a tailor, the shapes of the various structures seemed off to him. This wasn't the architecture he'd known back in England or the indigenous style of Outremer, either.

"God's nails," whispered Gaspard. Evidently he hadn't spotted anything familiar, either.

"This reminds me of the Forum in Rome," Ottomar murmured, "the place where many of the buildings from the time of the first Emperors still stand."

Pierangelo sneered. "Which is to say, pagan."

"Whatever it is," Gaspard said, "let's keep exploring. Maybe we'll find *something* that will help us." With that, they all prowled onward.

After a time, William veered around the fallen statue of a saintly-looking woman with one hand raised, perhaps in a sign of blessing, and the other missing. Then Pierangelo, who was leading the single-file procession, lifted his hand to signal a halt and ducked behind a pillar.

Everyone else took cover, too, although for a moment, William didn't know why. Then, crouching behind a block of stone with a weathered inscription on it, he heard what Pierangelo evidently had. Somewhere up ahead, it sounded like parchment was rustling. The cool night air was still at the moment, so there was no breeze to flutter paper, and the soft sound had an intermittent start-and-stop quality that somehow suggested purposeful movement.

Whatever the sound was, it didn't seem to be coming closer, and after a moment, Pierangelo gestured for his companions to gather around. Keeping his voice low, he asked, "Does anyone have any idea what we're hearing?"

Apparently no one did.

"Someone should scout ahead and find out," Gaspard said.

"Jibril," Ottomar said.

Pierangelo glowered. "I told you, I don't trust your Saracen."

"He's the best man for the task," Ottomar said.

Possibly Pierangelo would have retorted, but Jibril forestalled further argument by gliding forward. Watching as he disappeared into the darkness, William decided he probably was "the best man for the task." Unlike his companions, the Saracen wasn't wearing mail that might clink and give him away, but that wasn't the only reason for the utter silence of his progress. He moved like an expert hunter stalking prey.

Once Jibril was out of sight, the waiting gnawed at William's nerves. Eventually Pierangelo said, "He's abandoned us."

"Give him time," Ottomar replied, and shortly thereafter, the Saracen justified his confidence by returning. Jibril moved with the same noiseless grace as before, but his face had gone pale.

"What did you see?" Gaspard asked.

"A man," Jibril said, "made of parchment."

The Templar cocked his head. "You mean a drawing."

"No," Jibril said. "Moving. Alive."

Ottomar frowned. "You're overwrought, my friend. No shame in it. We all are."

The suggestion that he was imagining things brought some color back into Jibril's face and a frown to his lips. "I know it makes no sense, but I saw what I saw."

"He's lying," Pierangelo said, "and if he's not, I have to see for myself."

"You should not," Jibril said, but now it was Pierangelo's turn to advance without heeding. Gaspard and William stalked after their superior, and Ottomar followed along as well.

William half-expected Jibril, shaken by what he'd seen, his

courage and veracity impugned, to balk. But the Saracen took a long breath and then hurried up even with Pierangelo, presumably so he could lead him and the other knights to the "man made of parchment" by the most expeditious path.

The column skulked along quietly but without the perfect silence Jibril had achieved by himself. William's limbs felt stiff and clumsy, making it that much more difficult to tread stealthily, and his pulse beat in his neck.

He told himself there couldn't truly be a man made of parchment. Whoever had heard of such an absurdity? But now that he'd experienced one uncanny thing, a second didn't seem as unlikely as he would have wished, especially given the impression he'd formed of the Saracen during their combat. Jibril was cool-headed, not the sort of man to jump at shadows and return from a scouting foray prattling nonsense.

Unable to persuade himself there couldn't possibly be a man made of paper, William hit on the idea that even if such a flimsy creature existed, it couldn't possibly harm him. He was considering that notion and waiting to see if it would make him feel any less nervous when Jibril raised his hand to order another halt.

"Christ's precious heart," Ottomar breathed.

The men in front of him were blocking William's view. He stepped to the side, even though a part of him insisted he didn't truly want to behold what they were seeing.

A long stone's throw ahead of the column, a figure was prowling along a colonnade, visible in the spaces between columns, obscured when it moved behind one. Given the darkness and the distance, William couldn't see it all that well, but he discerned enough to make him shiver.

He'd imagined a creature that would be flat like a single sheet of parchment. The thing behind the pillars was indeed flattish, but not as flimsy and insubstantial as he'd supposed.

Most parts of its body were book-thick, seemingly made of multiple pieces of paper adhering together, which didn't keep it from bending and flopping as it shambled along. Stray scraps and corners had come loose from the rest of it, giving it a ragged, leprous appearance.

It had no eyes, ears, nose, or mouth on its disk of a head, but long tatters rose from the top to quiver and writhe. Some people might have taken them for hair or its counterfeit, but William suspected they were sensory organs somehow gathering impressions from the air.

Now that he was seeing the unnatural thing for himself, he was sure Jibril had been correct. The prudent course of action was for them to keep their distance and avoid detection.

"Demon." Pierangelo drew his sword.

"Don't be an idiot!" Ottomar said.

But apparently it was still a night when none of them was inclined to heed another's counsels. Pierangelo stepped out into a clearing between his former hiding space and the colonnade, and Gaspard and William unsheathed their blades and followed.

William anticipated that both Jibril and Ottomar would balk, but after a moment, he heard them bringing up the rear. His mouth dry, he wondered if they were prompted by honor, pride, or a coldblooded calculation that their chances of surviving this strange place were better if everyone acted as one, even when the action underway was folly.

Somehow, the parchment man sensed the swordsmen coming and turned to face them. The tatters atop its faceless head reared and lashed about, and after a few moments, to William's horror, other creatures of the same sort, each similarly covered in lines of text from head to foot, came bending and flopping out of the darkness. As reinforcements arrived, the first parchment man emerged from the shelter of the colonnade to join their advance.

Paper! William insisted to himself. *They're only made of paper!* He turned to face the one that was coming in on his flank, sprang forward in a move intended to take it by surprise, and slashed at its chest.

He'd cut at flesh and various types of armor before, but never at a dense stack of parchment. Either a sword was ill suited to the task, or some enchantment granted the creature's body a measure of resistance. The blade bit, but not as deeply as he expected, and afterward, no blood spurted, and the parchment man didn't falter, as if it didn't even notice the shallow slice.

Its fist leapt at him. He jumped back, but the blow still caught him in the belly and knocked the breath out of him. If not for his mail and the padding underneath, it might have hurt him worse than that.

His body wanted a moment to shake off the shock of the attack, but there wasn't one. The parchment man flailed at him, and he dodged until his strength returned and he was able to strike back.

He scored with more cuts, but the paper man didn't seem to notice them, either. He tried a thrust, and the point of his sword punched deeper. For an instant, he hoped that might be a good thing, and then his adversary rushed him and so plunged the blade through its body nearly all the way to the cross guard. He only barely managed to snatch the captured weapon free and, by dropping low, prevent the parchment man from gathering him into its arms.

As he and his foe circled, he caught glimpses of the other combatants and saw that while all his comrades were still on their feet, none of them had managed to fell a parchment man, either. *Fire!* he thought. Surely paper men would burn, but even if someone had the means to strike a flame, a parchment creature would surely dispatch him the moment he stopped fighting to go about it.

"The tatters!" Gaspard shouted. "Cut off the tatters on top of their heads!"

William tried that, and it proved to be a better tactic than anything he'd attempted hitherto. He could slash the writhing strips of parchment completely away, and when he did, his adversary froze for an instant as though finally feeling some distress.

Still, the tactic only slowed the paper man's onslaught a little. It wasn't enough to turn the fight around. There were at least a dozen tatters, and after he cut away two, the parchment man took care to protect the rest. It caught sword stroke after sword stroke on its upraised forearms, where the blade inflicted the usual shallow cuts but did no more.

William struggled to think of a ploy that would enable him and his companions to prevail. Then, as he and the parchment man circled, he saw, or thought he saw, something smooth and reflective on the ground. It was really only a different shade and texture of blackness amid the dark, but *perhaps* it was mirroring the stars.

Praying he wouldn't trip over something as he backed up, he retreated in that direction, and the parchment man pursued, still pressing him hard. He didn't like distancing himself from his comrades even though, busy with their own adversaries, they were in no position to help him anyway. But it had to be done.

He smelled water before he had his first close look at it. He circled, and, indeed, there was the pool he'd thought he saw. The builders of this forum had created it for some decorative, ceremonial, or practical purpose, and something still kept it filled.

By circling to face the pool, he'd also put the parchment

man's back to it. He dropped his sword, charged his foe, and wrapped his arms around its torso.

The creature immediately did the same thing to him with a terrible crushing strength. But he was bull rushing it backward, and they toppled over the edge of the pool and splashed in together.

In the dark, William had had no way of judging whether the pool was shallow or deep enough to keep a man from standing. Fortunately, it was shallow. He thrashed, his feet found the bottom, and he heaved his head up out of the water, registering as he did so that the potentially spine-snapping pressure across his back was abating to almost nothing. As he'd conjectured, water wasn't good for a parchment man. It turned the creature's substance mushy and weak.

He tore at the parchment man, and its body came apart. When he ripped the head away from the body, the thing stopped moving.

Gasping, he would gladly have clung to the side of the pool and rested for a while, but there wasn't any time, not if he was to keep everyone else alive. He clambered out of the water, recovered his sword, and ran back to the battleground where the others were fighting.

"Draw the creatures in this direction!" he shouted. "I found the way to kill them!"

He was relieved when everyone did as he'd bade them without questioning, relieved too that his call didn't appear to alert the parchment men that they were finally in real danger. Perhaps they couldn't hear or comprehend human speech, or else it was their nature to harry a foe relentlessly no matter the risk.

The black water was now spotted with floating pieces of the first parchment man's body. William and his fellows managed to shove in the others without anyone having to go in himself, then used their swords to beat their foes back rather than cutting the things apart. The final stage of the process proved to be relatively easy. The paper men became feeble as soon as they were immersed.

When the last one perished, the victors stood panting and regarding one another. William wondered if everyone felt as he did, glad to be alive, brotherly to the comrades who'd fought beside him, but still afflicted with a lingering horror at the demons.

After a few moments, Gaspard said, "I suppose they have to stay out of the rain." He clapped William on the shoulder. "Well done, lad."

"Yes," Pierangelo said.

"I agree," Ottomar said. His smile twisted into a frown when he turned to the Templar leader. "Which still doesn't mean it was intelligent to do battle in the first place."

"What do you think it means to be a knight?" Pierangelo replied. "What are you *for*?"

So much, William thought, *for brothers-in-arms.*

"Sirs," Gaspard said, "if I may, whether the fight was wise or unwise, it's over now. We have to decide what to do next. Do we keep exploring or return to Ox and the woman?"

Ottomar frowned as he abandoned his argument with Pierangelo to consider the question Gaspard had posed. "I think, return. There's no telling what else may be roaming about, and if there are landmarks we should recognize, I can't make them out in the dark. I'd rather seek shelter for the rest of the night and reconnoiter again by day."

Pierangelo gave a brusque nod. "That's reasonable."

As they retraced their steps, William found himself worrying they'd lose their way even though he could see the upper reaches of the building from which they'd departed. Plainly, it was impossible that they'd suddenly lose their bearings; except that was precisely a thing that often happened in his nightmares, and he'd never had a nightmare more disturbing than this.

Scowling, he pushed the irrational fear away. His time would be better spent watching out for more parchment men or other threats. Ottomar was right. Anything could be wandering around in the dark.

If there was something else, though, it didn't reveal itself as they made their way back, and in due course, William stepped back into the cathedral-like building with a sigh of relief. The place was part of the strangeness, but after the encounter with the parchment men, it felt like a refuge.

The orange lantern light revealed Ox sitting cross-legged on the floor with the bound woman lying before him and his unsheathed sword ready to hand. "Did she wake?" Ottomar asked. "Or has anything else happened?"

"No," Ox replied, and then the captive started writhing and bucking.

3

"She's calling on the Devil's strength to break her bonds!" Pierangelo said.

"No," Gaspard said, "or at least I don't believe so. I think it might be epilepsy. I knew someone who suffered from it."

Whatever ailed the prisoner, William was afraid she'd hurt herself thrashing on the hard stone floor or that she'd choke on the gag. "Can you help her?' he asked.

Gaspard shook his head. "I told you before, I'm no physician. We'll just have to wait for the seizure to pass."

Pierangelo drew his sword. "I'll 'wait' to strike her down if she frees herself, and I order the two of you to do the same."

The prisoner didn't break free. The seizure came to an end, and the eyes that had rolled up in her head rolled back down and shifted from side to side. She was aware of her surroundings again and proved it by trying to speak. The gag reduced her words to "Uh uh uh!"

"We'll have to ungag her to question her," Gaspard said.

"You're forgetting," Ottomar said, "she doesn't speak our language."

"I didn't forget," Gaspard replied, "but we didn't try every language any of us knows, did we? Even if it just turns out that one of us knows a few words of a particular tongue, and she does, too, that will be better than nothing."

Ottomar grunted. "When you put it that way, I agree."

"Well, I haven't," Pierangelo said.

The senior Hospitaler gave his counterpart a sour look. "We relieved her of her grimoire, if that's what is frightening you. We're going to keep her tied up. Surely you'll be able to act first if she tries to cast a spell on you. Don't you think that and your faith will suffice to protect you?"

"And, sir," Gaspard said, "if we *aren't* going to try questioning her, what plan should we pursue instead?"

Pierangelo glowered at Ox. "Ungag her. But be ready to act on my command."

Ox looked to Ottomar, who gave him a nod. "You might as well help her sit up, too."

When the gag came out, the prisoner swallowed twice. Then she spoke, and William gasped as he felt a momentary squirming sensation behind his eyes, as though worms were crawling around inside his head. When the feeling passed, he realized he could understand two of the words the woman was saying, not because she'd switched to a different language but because he suddenly had some knowledge of the one she'd been using all along.

He looked around at the other knights and Jibril. Judging from their stunned expressions, they'd all experienced the same thing he had.

The captive waited for a moment and then, evidently realizing she hadn't made herself fully understood, repeated what she'd said before. This time, William comprehended all of it.

"Is the spell of tongues working?" she asked.

"I told you it was a spell!" Pierangelo said.

"At least it was a helpful one," Gaspard said. A bit haltingly, he switched to the same language the prisoner was speaking, whereupon William realized he could now speak it too if he saw fit. "Who are you?"

"Kolinda Deepwell," the woman said. She had a bruise coming up on her cheek where Gaspard had pinched her. "Your friend. Truly."

"And what is this place?" Ottomar asked.

"The temple of Anjalor in Phon," Kolinda said.

The six men exchanged glances. From their expressions, no one had ever heard of such places. "Pagan," Pierangelo said in Latin.

Ottomar looked back at the woman sitting on the floor, then hesitated. William didn't blame him. He had so many questions that he wouldn't have known which one to ask next, either.

The senior Hospitaler settled on, "How did we get here?"

"I summoned you," the prisoner said, a trace of pride or at least satisfaction in her voice. "With a passage from Daran's *Meditations*."

"Then…you can return us to Acre?"

Kolinda's eyes widened as though the question had startled her. "What? No. The book doesn't provide for that, and even if it did, you're meant to be here."

Gaspard squatted down beside her, putting them eye to eye, and gave her a smile. "We could be at this all night, peck-peck-pecking away with questions. Why don't you tell us the whole story? Assume we know nothing about this country and what's going on here, because that's exactly the case."

Kolinda cocked her head. "Nothing at all? I assumed…but no, it makes sense that you don't." She paused for a moment, seemingly ordering her thoughts. "There are the Western Kingdoms, where people worship the kindly gods and cherish virtue. Well, sometimes, anyway. That's where I'm from. And there are the Stained Lands, where people bow down to demons and practice sorcery."

"Wait," Gaspard said. "Didn't you use sorcery to bring us here?"

The prisoner hesitated. "A different kind. It's complicated."

"All right. Keep going."

"Long ago, a mystic named Daran the Blind foresaw that one day, there would be a great war between West and East. He said that when that happened, goodness could prevail, but only if a band of holy warriors traveled from their world to this one and became the champions of my people. Accordingly, he set down a spell to summon you.

"Daran didn't explain why," Kolinda continued, "at least not in terms I understand, but the spell could only work here. Perhaps it has something to do with this being the place where the two worlds touch, or the particular power that manifests in the temple. Be that as it may, the great war *is* coming. The signs are clear. So I slipped into the Stained Lands, found the proper location, read the passage from the book, and here you are!"

With that, she gave her captors a bright smile that appeared to convey her hope that, now that she'd explained, they were all friends and the men would recognize she'd done something splendid. The knights and Jibril eyed her and one another uncertainly.

William supposed that, by swearing the vows they took, Templars and Hospitalers did become "holy warriors" in a legalistic sense, but of the knights Kolinda had summoned, only Pierangelo might arguably fit the description in actuality. Perhaps Daran's magic hadn't chosen with any great perceptiveness or precision. It had, after all, seemingly scooped up Jibril the Saracen just because he was in proximity to the others.

Kolinda's smile wilted a little even though she was clearly trying to hold on to it. "So you can untie me now," she said.

"First we have to confer," Ottomar said. "Ox, please stay with her. The rest of you, join me over here." He led them to a spot midway between the prisoner and her guard and the exit.

"It isn't really necessary to distance ourselves from her to keep her from eavesdropping," Gaspard said, reverting to Latin. "She cast a spell to teach us her language, not the other way around."

Ottomar raised an eyebrow. "Are you an authority on sorcery now, to be quite certain of that?"

Gaspard grinned. "All right, that's fair enough." Quick as it had appeared, the smile gave way to a more serious expression. "How much of what we just heard do we believe?"

William blinked. "I thought...all of it?"

Pierangelo gave him a withering glower that suggested he'd now expended any credit he'd earned by figuring out how to defeat the parchment men. "None of it, fool! She admitted she's a witch. Why, then, would you believe a word she says?"

"Other than our distrust of witches," Gaspard said, "do we have a reason to think her story *isn't* true?"

"Yes!" Pierangelo said, pouncing much as he might have lunged to strike through an opening in an opponent's guard. "She claims to have called us from our own world into a different one. God only created one world. Or aren't you familiar with Genesis?"

"I am, sir," Gaspard said, "and of course I know we aren't literally in a different *world*. We're in some land so far removed from our own that none of us ever heard of it before. But perhaps she didn't intend to mislead us. The spell of tongues may not work perfectly. It's possible we even heard 'spell' when she meant 'prayer.'"

"She spoke of 'gods,'" the older man replied, "not God. At the very least, that makes her pagan, and if her 'prayer' was answered, it was by Hell whether she knows it or not."

"I see your point," Ottomar said, "but it doesn't answer the question I want to discuss. Should we believe her when she says she can't send us back to Acre?"

William was reluctant to speak up again. He seemed to invite Pierangelo's scorn every time he did. Still, he said, "I didn't have the feeling she was lying."

"Nor did I," Gaspard said, "and I was close enough to study her face. But that could just mean she's a *good* liar, and if she brought us here to fight in her war, she may think it will help persuade us if we believe there's no way of going home."

"So you finally recognize what I've been saying all along," Pierangelo said. "If we want the truth, we need to wring it out of her."

"If we torture her," Gaspard said, "we'll make an enemy of someone who thus far seems to hold us in high regard even though we took her prisoner. Someone who's our only source of information and who may have done nothing wrong."

The senior Templar sneered. "Witchcraft and abduction aren't wrong?"

"Sir," William said, even though he once again suspected the course of wisdom was to keep his mouth shut, "you're the one who led the rest of us against the parchment men. If her story *is* true, don't you *want* to help her?"

"Do you?" Pierangelo replied.

"Well...I might."

To William's surprise, the older knight's stern expression softened a little. Perhaps this was one of the rare occasions when he judged that something other than barked commands and snarled rebukes was needed to motivate his underlings to good effect.

"Of course we fought the demons," Pierangelo said, "when God's will put them right in front of us. But as far as this 'great war' is concerned, as I keep reminding the rest of you, Kolinda Deepwell is a pagan. It's impossible for any pagan cause to be just or righteous. Surely you see that."

"I suppose," William said.

"But there *is* a righteous struggle underway, the struggle to unite all the Holy Land under the banner of Christ, the struggle you've sworn a sacred oath to support. You must see, then, that it's our duty to return to our proper place as quickly as possible."

William supposed that made sense even though, during his time in Outremer, he'd seen precious little done to advance that righteous struggle. "Yes, sir," he said.

Pierangelo's usual cold, grim demeanor snapped back into place. "Make sure you remember it, then."

"I think we're all in agreement," Ottomar said, "that we want to return to Acre as quickly as possible. The question is, how to deal with Kolinda to achieve that. Putting her to the question may or may not be the best approach. Perhaps we should pretend to trust her and see what develops."

"What if," Gaspard said, "the spell of tongues allows us not just to speak her language but to read it? We have the *Meditations*. We could study it for ourselves and see if it actually does contain the magic to send us home. If so, we could force Kolinda to recite the incantation or even try reciting it ourselves."

"The buyers of magic have no share in the Hereafter,"

Jibril said. The Saracen was usually so quiet that it half-startled William to hear him speak.

"On that one point," Pierangelo said, "we agree."

"But as you pointed out, sir," Gaspard said, "it's our duty to return home. I'm willing to read the book, even read a bit of it aloud, if that's what it takes."

"I think that's sensible," Ottomar said. "I believe that under the circumstances, God would forgive you."

"Do you believe it strongly enough to read it yourself," Pierangelo asked, "and endanger your own soul?"

The senior Hospitaler sighed in a way that conveyed he was being patient in the face of foolishness or provocation. "If Sir Gaspard does end up studying the book, I doubt it will give up its secrets quickly. We need to decide what to do right now. Do we deal with the woman gently or severely?"

"Let's try gently," Gaspard said, "for a little longer, anyway. We can always turn to force if it becomes clear that's not getting us anywhere."

To William's relief, the others acquiesced, although it was clear Pierangelo wasn't prepared to refrain from brutality much longer. Gaspard walked back to Kolinda, squatted beside her, and, switching back to her language, said, "We have a few more questions."

"Anything," Kolinda replied.

"You told us this is a holy place."

"Of course." She eyed Gaspard uncertainly. "Being what you are, surely you feel the purity and the glory here."

The Templar hesitated. Then: "In all honesty, no. We don't feel a thing, and while you were unconscious, we—all of us but Ox here—went outside for a look around. We met things shaped like men but made of parchment and had to fight them. I don't know exactly what they were, but I'm fairly sure they weren't holy in any sense of the word."

Kolinda goggled at him. "We have to get away from here right away!"

"Why?" Gaspard asked. "We can't untie you or go where you lead until we understand."

For a moment, the prisoner looked like she wanted to scream at him. Then she mastered herself and continued speaking softly, though the words came more rapidly.

"When the Stain ran through these lands, there were a few places so sacred that it couldn't get in. Anjalor's memory likewise deters some of the servants bred of the Stain from coming in—it pains them—and the demon lords don't want their human worshippers exploring here, either. The holiness might spark the realization that there's a better way to live. But even so, *something* must patrol from time to time to discourage relic hunters or pilgrims from the West."

"So to attend to that, some sorcerer made the parchment men?"

"Yes, desecrating and destroying sacred texts for the purpose. That's the Eastern sense of humor."

"All right," William said, "but we killed the parchment men."

Gaspard glanced around at him. "Someone sent them and will miss them when they don't return on schedule."

"Then he'll send a larger force," Jibril said. "Or surround this place. Or both. It could be happening already."

"Exactly," Kolinda said. "Let me lead you to safety while there's still time."

"We need to confer again," Ottomar said, "for just a moment longer."

"You don't *have* a moment!" Kolinda said. But she could do nothing to prevent them from distancing themselves from her as they had before.

"Well, "Ottomar asked, "do we believe her now?"

"It's an outlandish story," Gaspard said, "but it fits the

outlandish things that have happened to us, and if it isn't true, what is?"

"Your faith," Pierangelo said.

"Yes, sir," Gaspard said, "of course. But we don't have to accept Kolinda's claims to virtue to believe there truly is a war happening and that if we don't want to deal with a bigger force of parchment men or worse, we need to get away from this place."

"If she leads us away from here," Ottomar said, "she may be leading us away from the only place from which the magic could return us to Acre…but I don't think she's tricking us, or *only* tricking us. Her fear seems real."

"It's settled, then," Ottomar said, perhaps before Pierangelo could demur. "Ox!" he called. "Untie her. We're leaving."

When freed, Kolinda stood up stiffly and rubbed her hands together, likely to rid them of the numbness or stinging having one's extremities bound could produce. Then she cast about, spied the knife, mace, and book where Gaspard had set them, and started toward them.

"Leave those!" Pierangelo snapped.

"Ox will carry them for you," Ottomar said.

Kolinda scowled. "You fought the parchment men and you *still* don't believe me?"

"It's just for the moment," the senior Hospitaler said. "I'm sure we'll be able to return them soon."

William thought that if she argued further, it would be to take custody of what she plainly regarded as a holy book, but she surprised him. "Your man can carry the *Meditations* for now. As long as it isn't left behind. But I need a way to defend myself. Or are you afraid the one of me could overcome the six of you?"

Gaspard grinned. "We hope not." He turned to Pierangelo. "Sir, if we do have to fight, we might be glad she's armed."

"Very well," the senior Templar growled, "but Ox *will* hold onto the book until I say otherwise."

William suspected that of all of them, Ox might be the least able to read Daran's *Meditations* and make any sense of it. He also suspected that might be just as Pierangelo wanted it.

4

As far as William could tell, nothing was lurking beyond the door. Still, he said, "Wait." Then, when everyone turned to look at him, he almost wished he hadn't.

Gaspard gave him a smile. "Go on. If you've thought of something, we want to hear it."

"It's just...in the tales I heard growing up, goblins and such come out at night. So perhaps we should stay where we are until sunrise."

"I can see why you'd say that," said Kolinda, now wrapped in a gray hooded cloak of her own with a knapsack slung over her shoulder. "Some Stained creatures do see or otherwise sense things very well in the dark. The parchment men are one example. That's another reason their master used them to patrol here. But the lords of the East also have plenty of servants who are hindered by darkness and prefer daylight."

"So there's nothing to gain and potentially much to lose by waiting for dawn," Gaspard said. He peered beyond the doorway one last time and then stepped warily through. The others followed.

"Are there horses?" William asked, looking about. He hadn't noticed any sign of them before, but he and the other men had gone exploring in only one direction.

"No," Kolinda said. "Even if I could have managed a whole string of them, it would have made me too conspicuous traveling in this country. We'll have to walk out."

"Then let's get to it," Gaspard said. "West, I assume." He studied the sky and then muttered, "God's nails."

"What's wrong?" William asked.

"Wherever this place is," Gaspard said, "it's so far from home that the stars themselves are different. I can't find north."

"I told you," Kolinda said, "you've traveled to a whole different world from...never mind. There isn't time to go through it all again. West is this way. Come on, and be quiet."

With that, she led her companions onward through a maze of ruinous buildings that might once have been temples, too, albeit lesser ones than the imposing hall they were leaving and to which, as best William could judge, they might never return. It troubled him to abandon what might be the only door between this land and Outremer; it troubled him too that he and his fellows were dependent on the guidance of a self-confessed witch none of them trusted.

But he and his companions had decided on a course of action, they were pursuing it, and there was nothing to be gained from fretting while they found out where it would lead them. Perhaps this experience would turn out to be the grand adventure he'd imagined being a Crusader would be before discovering the disappointing reality, and surely the instinct that told him Kolinda was a good person couldn't be altogether wrong.

The vague black shapes of the buildings became smaller

as the procession crept along, and the statues, fallen or otherwise, less frequent. Maybe, William thought, they'd entered a part of the complex given over to living quarters for the lesser priests, and dormitories and workshops for the many laborers who had likely once been necessary to keep the place running, and thus there had been less effort invested here to impress pilgrims visiting the temples.

Eventually he and his companions reached a spot from which he could make out open country through the spaces between buildings. They all quickened their steps, and then Jibril, who was walking at the head of procession alongside Kolinda, spun, lifted his hands to signal everyone to stop, and then waved them in a gesture that conveyed *Get down*, or, interpreted more broadly, *take cover*.

There was a small structure on William's right. As he scurried over and crouched behind it, he registered that it was a dilapidated well house. He peered around the side of it to see what had alarmed the Saracen.

Even in the dark, the somewhat hound-like beast wasn't difficult to spot. It was as big as a cottage, and perhaps that was why some demon or sorcerer maker had given it an extra pair of legs midway down the long body: to help it manage its weight. Its head was mostly oversized jaws and snout, with cropped ears and a single cyclopean eye, and it *sniff-sniff-sniffed* as it paced along. There were two men walking with it, but, appalled by the creature, William scarcely paid them any mind.

Please pass on by, he thought, and then an alarming possibility occurred to him.

Pierangelo had deemed himself honor-bound to fight the parchment men. Would he think duty obliged him to confront this new monstrosity as well? William cast about in an effort to find his superior's hiding place.

Pierangelo had taken cover behind a weathered obelisk.

He was peering out at the creature with a scowl that conveyed loathing but no fear, and his right hand was clenched on the hilt of his sword. But he wasn't *drawing* the weapon or striding out into the open, and for that, William was grateful. The huge hound was going to pass on by without detecting them.

Except that it didn't. It nearly did, but then it swung its long body around in the Crusaders' direction, and the minders walking by its forepaws had to scramble to keep the sudden pivot from knocking them over. The beast sniffed more vigorously than before.

"Is someone there?" called one of the minders. He was speaking a different language than Kolinda's, but the spell of tongues apparently rendered this new one comprehensible as well. "If so, I advise you to show yourself. No? Your choice, then. Go get him, boy!"

The hound stalked forward. Pierangelo took a deep breath and squared his shoulders. Plainly, if the beast was coming anyway, he preferred to step forth to meet it rather than have it ferret him out.

Then, however, as the one-eyed creature started to pass between two of the structures on the edge of the complex, it yelped and flinched.

Ottomar whispered a single word from wherever he was hiding in the darkness. "Wait!" And Pierangelo did.

"Go!" said the minder who'd spoken before. "Catch!" The hound still balked. "Catch, or I'll use the rod!" The creature rounded on him with a growl, and the minder took a hasty step backward.

"Pain or no," the second minder said, the hint of a quaver in his voice, "he would have gone in if there was really a tres-passer and not just a rabbit or something like that. Let's not force the issue."

"We can't let him get in the habit of thinking he can

disobey," the first minder said. "But...maybe this isn't the moment. We've walked nearly all the way around, and I'm hungry." He met the glare of the hound's single eye. "All right, Ripper, I won't scourge you this time. But if there's no one to find, move on!" He pointed, and he, his partner, and the beast continued on their way just beyond the perimeter of the complex.

When they were gone, Ottomar came closer to Pierangelo and said, "Thank God you're not completely devoid of sense."

"I know what I should have done," the Templar replied, "but you, you pitiful excuse for a knight, you of all people have no right to mock me."

"Please," Kolinda said, "there'll be time enough to destroy the One-Eyed Hounds and all the other Stained horrors when you have the armies of the West under your command. But for now, we really must keep moving."

They did move, into a moor of low hills. In time, the first gray and purple signs of dawn appeared in the sky at their backs. William felt a vague relief that he too could now say of his own knowledge that they were heading west. It made him feel marginally less helpless.

Kolinda called a halt, passed around a leather bottle full of tepid water, and shared out brown bread and a sharp yellow cheese from her knapsack. The food didn't taste quite like any bread or cheese William had had before, and although the loaf was stale, everything was palatable enough. They all took a short rest, and then the witch urged them on.

Gaspard fell in beside her. "Are you able to keep this pace?" he asked.

She brushed away an insect that was fluttering around her face, or so William assumed. He could actually see it, not in the feeble predawn light from several paces away. "Why wouldn't I be?" she asked.

"At one point during the night, you had a seizure."

Kolinda shook her head. "I can understand how it looked that way, but no. Sorcery is more of a strain than I expected. When I had to cast a second spell, the spell of tongues, I fainted." She hesitated. "It seemed as though my spirit left my body, and I had to struggle with...*something* to get back in. But maybe that part was only a dream. It's already faded like a dream."

"You don't talk like an all-powerful mistress of witchcraft."

"Because I'm not. In better times, it never would have occurred me to study the *Meditations* with the goal of casting spells." She snorted. "From the way you and the others have treated me, I imagine you're glad I'm not a real sorceress."

"Well...according to Christian teachings, witchcraft is evil. I believe that even Jibril's religion says the same."

Catching his name, the wiry, black-bearded Saracen glanced over and gave Kolinda and the Templar a cool nod.

"But I confess," Gaspard continued "when I see something like parchment men or a One-Eyed Hound, it's tempting to wish we had magic to strike them down. If King Arthur could have Merlin, it seems like we should be able to call on someone comparable." He smiled. "Although I take it that even though you're trying to avoid trouble, you believe that if we mighty champions do have to fight, we shouldn't need any help."

Kolinda swiped at another insect, or perhaps the first one still flitting stubbornly around her. "You're not what I expected," she said. "You don't trust me or even one another, and you don't want to undertake your sacred mission. Nor did you feel the power in Anjalor's holy shrine. Even I could feel it, and I've sworn only the lesser vows of my sisterhood."

Gaspard cocked his head. "You're a nun?"

"I don't know that word," she replied, and William realized the word *nun* had come out in Latin, perhaps because

Kolinda's language lacked a counterpart. "I'm a priestess, but of a clerkish kind. I do my best to keep worms from eating old books, take dictation, and copy manuscripts. I don't preach or tend to the poor and the sick."

Gaspard mulled that over for a moment, then returned to the previous point. "Well, if my companions and I aren't what you were fishing for, I can only say we never pretended to be. You're the only person who's claimed we have some sort of noble destiny hereabouts."

Kolinda sighed. "I know, and it's easy enough to believe I blundered somehow. After all, who am I to attempt magic? Except...the spell was supposed to bring six warriors, and it did. Then you defeated the parchment men, and the One-Eyed Hound wouldn't come after us even though it has a vicious temperament and that's exactly what it's been trained to do. It all has to mean *something*."

"We might not have overcome the paper men if young William over there wasn't cleverer that he gives himself credit for," Gaspard replied. The praise made William feel both proud and embarrassed, but he kept on pretending he wasn't eavesdropping and hadn't heard. "The giant dog may have been less fierce or less well trained than average, and as its minders said themselves, they were more interested in finishing their patrol and getting supper than in trying to force it to do what it didn't want to do and maybe getting bitten in two for their pains."

Kolinda shook her head. "I have faith that there's more to it than that. I..."

Somewhere behind them—distantly, but, William feared, not distant enough—horns blared and shrilled.

"What's that?" asked Ox, in a blithe tone that suggested he didn't realize the clamor might signify anything that need concern them.

"Someone found the remains of the parchment men,"

Kolinda replied, "or happened upon some other evidence of our intrusion, and now the Easterners are sounding the alarm."

5

"Will they come after us?" William asked.

Pierangelo gave him another scornful look. "Clearly."

"Have we traveled far enough to stay ahead of them?" Gaspard asked.

Kolinda shook her head. "I doubt it. Not on foot."

"Then what," Ottomar asked, "is your plan for dealing with this situation?"

"I don't have one," the priestess replied. "I hoped we'd sneak out without being noticed." Her companions frowned, or exchanged looks of chagrin, and her tone grew sharper. "I told you, I haven't done this sort of thing before!"

"If we can't outdistance them," Pierangelo said, "we stand and fight."

Gaspard scratched his chin through his beard. "An ambush might work."

"What if there are too many of them?" Ottomar asked. "What if they bring a dozen of those dog creatures?"

Pierangelo made a spitting sound. "Then better to die fighting than be run down like a deer."

"There might," said Jibril, "be another way. We can lay a false trail."

"Will we have time to do that," Gaspard asked, "before the chase catches up with us?"

The Saracen shrugged. "If Allah wills."

Pierangelo scowled at the mention of the Islamic deity. Gaspard, however, grinned and said, "In other words, it's a gamble. Understood. I think we should try."

"As do I," Ottomar said.

"Then we should keep moving for now," Jibril said, "and find a place where the ground is better."

That place turned out to be a spot where the earth was hard and the brush was light, just a little farther down the trail.

"Some will wait and stand guard here," Jibril said. "One or two will come with me to help make footprints and other signs."

Ox smiled. "I can make footprints!"

Ottomar turned to Kolinda. "Perhaps you should help, too. All our boot prints look much the same, but yours are different. Smaller. If our pursuers are looking for them and fail to find them, they could detect the ruse."

Kolinda nodded. "I understand."

She, Ox, and Jibril moved off into an area of soft ground and thicker brush. Periodically the brush rustled or snapped when the Saracen bent or broke some of it to make the false trail clearer.

Meanwhile, the morning was quickly becoming hot. William and the other knights keeping watch found places to sit or lean, sweated, and squinted in the direction of the rising sun. As far as he could tell, their pursuers weren't on the verge of catching up, and after a time, he stretched his arms out before him to inspect the sleeves of his coat of mail. He hadn't had the time or the means to care for it after he and the parchment man had plunged into the pool together, and while he supposed the thought was foolish, it bothered him to think that he might fight his last fight in rusty armor.

Breaking the silence, Gaspard said, "Someday I want to know exactly who and what Jibril is."

"We have more important things to talk about," Ottomar said, keeping his voice low. Mail clinking, he looked over his shoulder, and William surmised he was making sure the trio laying the false trail had moved out of earshot. "We've been saying that in this situation, we can either fight or flee, but what if there's a better option than either?"

"Look in the book of magic?" Gaspard asked.

Ottomar shook his head. "Even if the spell to return us home is in there, it likely isn't something one of us can cast easily. Otherwise Kolinda would have put up more of a fight about handing it over. But there are other sorcerers in this game."

Gaspard cocked his head. "You mean our pursuers."

"Yes," the senior Hospitaler said, "and Kolinda said they're *real* witches and warlocks whereas she's just a neophyte. It may well be, then, that they have the means to send us back to Acre, and as you said yourself, Pierangelo, a quarrel between two pagan peoples is none of our affair. Why, then, shouldn't we come to an understanding with Kolinda's enemies?"

"I imagine," Gaspard said, "that understanding would necessarily involve handing over Kolinda."

"Would that be so awful?" Ottomar asked. "She abducted us, and 'thou shalt not suffer a witch to live.'"

"Unless the witch is in a position to do you a favor?" Gaspard replied.

For a moment, Ottomar's mouth shut tight in exasperation. "If we don't traffic with someone's magic sometime, how are we ever going to return home?"

"Determine the proper direction," Pierangelo said, "and start riding. Or sailing as the case may be."

"Who's to say how many months or years that would take?" the Knight of the Hospital said. "Maybe you're content to leave your duties unattended for that long, but I'm not."

William cleared his throat. "I…I know I'm the youngest and have seen the least of everyone here. Perhaps I should keep quiet and wait to do as I'm told. But…do we truly see no difference between Kolinda and the power that makes parchment men and breeds One-Eyed Hounds?"

Gaspard gave him a nod. "That's a good question, but the answer may not be as plain as you suppose. The creatures are unnatural horrors, but the men who were in charge of the One-Eyed Hound didn't reek of evil. They just seemed like any pair of not-very-diligent soldiers to me."

William felt vaguely betrayed. He'd imagined Gaspard at least would see his point of view. "Then you're with Sir Ottomar?" he asked.

"Patience," Gaspard replied. "I'm simply weighing *all* the facts before making a decision. And, having done so, I think we should continue as we've been going." He looked to Ottomar. "Sir, it was your idea that we go along with Kolinda for the time being and see what happens. It's bad practice to jump from plan to plan to plan without good reason."

"Our pursuers may be an excellent reason," Ottomar said, "but if none of you are with me…?"

"I despise what Kolinda is," Pierangelo said, "and I won't dishonor my faith and my vows by pretending otherwise. But I won't go humbly begging favors from some other devil worshippers, either."

The senior Hospitaler sighed. "That settles it, then."

William found himself wondering if it only settled it until Ox and Jibril returned to side with Ottomar and the latter seized on an opportunity. Then he chided himself for his mistrust. Surely in this mad situation, the one thing he *could* rely on was the word of a Christian knight to his fellows.

Not long after, their companions returned. "We left tracks until we came to harder ground," Jibril said, "where hunters might expect to lose a trail. Now we go this way." He pointed off at a right angle to the course the fugitives had followed hitherto.

6

A   t midday, they stopped for another rest in a wood
        where the cedars and pines should shield them
        from the eyes of anyone peering from a distance.
Though he had no doubt it was prudent, William wondered
if they even needed to hide. After that first blaring of horns,
there'd been no further signs of pursuit.

"Maybe the false trail really did fool them," he said.

"I hope so," Gaspard answered, "but the shortcoming of a
false trail is that it can only lead so far, and when they lose it,
dedicated pursuers will cast about and possibly discern
where we actually went. Or just spread out across the countryside looking for us."

"That last," said Ottomar, wiping sweat from his brow,
"presumes a large number of hunters and a fair amount of
dedication."

"True." Gaspard said, "but we did kill their parchment
men." He looked to Kolinda. "How much will that concern
them?"

"Hm." She paused to consider with the thoughtful,
narrow-eyed expression that, William had decided, was as

characteristic of her as Gaspard's crooked smile, Ottomar's look of avuncular amiability, and Ox's appearance of placid unconcern were of them. "They'll understand it took warriors to destroy a patrol of parchment men. That will worry them more than if a simple worshipper or two sneaked into Anjalor's temple to pray. And if some sorcerer can tell I worked magic there, that will trouble them most of all."

"This is what troubles me," Jibril said. They'd been passing the water bottle around, and when the others turned to look at him, the Saracen upended it. Only a drop fell out. "Judging from the size of your knapsack, Kolinda, I assume food is likewise in short supply."

"I'm afraid so," the priestess said. "I could only carry so much."

"And after all," Gaspard said, "if we were mighty heroes capable of winning a war for you, we should certainly be up to the task of procuring rations. But now that you've seen the less impressive reality, are we better off foraging or simply pressing on until we cross over into your Western kingdoms?"

She hesitated. "I knew how I intended to take you west. I knew what we could find along the way. But now that we've deviated from our course by laying the false trail and turning north to throw off pursuit...well, with any luck, we should come upon streams eventually, but we may want to get more food."

"I did a fair amount of hunting back in Devon," William said. "If I had a bow or a crossbow—"

"But you don't," Pierangelo snapped.

"Nor can we afford the time for a day's hunting," Gaspard said. He smiled at William. "Not a bad thought nonetheless, but for now, I think we simply keep moving and keep an eye out for berries and those streams Kolinda mentioned."

As the day wore on, William's throat grew dry, and he looked for water and berries—which would presumably be juicy—with increasing avidity. Unfortunately, only the latter appeared, and though the fruit looked like wild raspberries to him, Kolinda cried out that they were poisonous an instant before Ox would otherwise have stuffed a handful in his mouth.

Eventually Kolinda decided to lead them due west again, or as near to due west as the vagaries of the terrain would allow, and they marched with the setting sun in their eyes. Half dazzled, it took William a moment to discern why those trudging along before him had stopped when they climbed to the top of a rise. Below them, scrubland and patches of woods gave way to fields and pastures with a cluster of huts in the center.

"Your mother's grave," the priestess said. From her disgusted tone, William inferred she was swearing. "We should have turned sooner. Now we'll have to backtrack. Or creep along the edge of the farmland."

"Wait," Ottomar said. "Let's think about this. We need food and water. The people below must have them."

"That doesn't mean they'll share," Kolinda said.

Pierangelo snorted. "They're peasants, not men-at-arms."

"I know," she replied. "I also know they're the enemies of my people, and getting you six to the West matters more than anything. But imagine if just one of them runs away to seek help."

"We know our business," the senior Templar said. "No one will tell what he saw, not while it's happening and not afterward, either."

"I'm sure you're right, sir," Gaspard said, "but the site of a massacre can tell a story all by itself. Perhaps there's a better way. What if we pass ourselves off as something we're not?"

Pierangelo sneered. "I wouldn't walk a step in this foul place without my sword and mail."

"Nor would I." Gaspard turned to Kolinda. "But could we impersonate soldiers in service to the sorcerer lords?"

She pondered the question, then said, "Perhaps. If you let me do the talking. They won't have seen armor like yours before or the crosses on your trappings, either, but humble folk shouldn't expect to know all there is to know about all the martial orders fighting for the Stain."

"I believe we should try," Jibril said, "and if it doesn't work, we'll still have our swords."

Pierangelo scowled. "I don't like the idea of claiming to be anything other than the servant of Jesus Christ I truly am."

Jibril turned his hands palms upward. "Disguise is a weapon like any other. A most effective one under the right circumstances."

"The farmers might even have horses we can commandeer," Ottomar said.

"All right," Pierangelo gritted, "just this once."

With Kolinda in the lead, they headed down the far slope. Surveying the pastures, William didn't see any horses, but there was a cow and some sheep. It was marginally reassuring that they looked normal. The cow had two eyes, and none of the rams nor ewes were enormous with an extra pair of legs.

Before long, a man working in the fields caught sight of the newcomers, raised a shout, and then ran toward the cluster of huts. Other peasants scurried in the same direction. With his heart beating faster, William hoped they weren't all rushing to prepare some sort of defense. It seemed unlikely, but in this place, who knew what to expect?

His anxiety became a little stronger, a little harder to hide from his companions, when they reached level ground and the crops growing in the fields somewhat obscured their view of whatever was transpiring ahead. Still, the modest prosperity of his father's small fief had depended on agriculture, and he reflexively noticed that the wheat and rye, fall crops both, were nearly ready to harvest, and when that sank in, it was shocking. Yesterday it had been spring in Acre. He wondered if, along with the altered constellations, the discrepancy in time meant that he, his fellow knights, and Jibril really had traveled to an entirely new world. But no, surely not. Pierangelo was far wiser than he, and the elder Templar said the idea was nonsense.

William also noticed the harvest would be poor this season. The crops as a whole looked stunted, and something brown and slimy grew on some of the heads. For a moment, he felt sorry for the folk who were likely to have a hungry winter. Then, trying to emulate Pierangelo's hardness, he reminded himself he had his own troubles to contend with.

Eventually the path among the fields provided another clear view of the collection of huts and the open space in the middle of them. Two dozen villagers—pretty much all of them, he suspected—had gathered there, but not with weapons in hand or with some ferocious creature to unleash. To the contrary: from their servile demeanors, they seemed poised to offer a formal greeting to people they believed held authority over them.

Kolinda stalked forward. *She* was pretty good at feigning arrogance, better than William would have expected from anything she'd done hitherto. "I'm Coldbreath," she said, "coven-daughter to Lady Sweethreath. Who's in charge?"

A stooped man with thinning grizzled hair bent over still farther in a show of subservience. "I am, lady," he said. Straightening up again to the extent he was able, he said, "Bring them forth."

The ranks of villagers started to part, opening an aisle, William realized, for people who'd been waiting on the other side to enter on cue. But those others were too impatient to wait for their fellows to make way. They pushed their way through, and no one raised a hand or otherwise objected, even when a woman fell and the baby in her arms started crying.

To William's surprise, the two bullies were still children, or at least he thought they might be. The one in the lead, who'd done the greater part of the shoving, was nearly as tall as he was and broader across the shoulders but still had the proportions of a toddler and pimples dotting the round face below the wispy hair. The one bringing up the rear had the body of a boy of ten or so but the wrinkled features and malicious superior smirk of some elderly miser.

"Masters," the stooped man said, in the manner of one reciting from a prepared text, "we welcome you and offer the first fruits of the harvest. This year, we are blessed. The gods touched two of our children."

William didn't understand. He glanced at Kolinda and realized from a look of uncertainty on her face that she wasn't sure what to make of this complication, either.

She collected herself quickly, though. "We didn't come to collect the, uh, tribute. Someone will be along for that later. We're hunting fugitives who trespassed in the ruins a day's travel to the east." She glowered at the assembled villagers. "Has anyone seen any strangers?"

No one spoke up.

Ottomar stepped up beside Kolinda and said, "My lady, this is as good a place as we're likely to find to spend the night."

After a moment's hesitation, the priestess said, "I agree." She looked back at the stooped man. "Bring us water, and cook us a proper supper. We'll also need you and your family to clear out of your hut."

"Yes, lady." He waved his hand, and some of the villagers

scurried off, presumably to start obeying Kolinda's commands. But others lingered, and the elder himself seemed to have more he wanted to say.

"What is it?" Kolinda snapped.

"I just thought…if you *did* take the boys with you when you leave, they could be useful and start serving Lady Sweetbreath all the sooner. And it would be a kindness—" The youth with the wrinkled face leered at him, and he faltered. "I mean, we're just eager to do our duty."

"I haven't the time nor the inclination to look after children," Kolinda said. That made the wrinkled boy frown. "I told you, someone will be along to collect them later. Now where's our water?"

Somebody offered a bucket, and others, a miscellany of cups they'd fetched from their homes. When it was William's turn to dip and drink, the water was cold and eased his parched throat. For that one moment, slaking his thirst made this experience feel as if it weren't such a nightmare after all.

"Next, our hut," Kolinda said. "Don't disturb us until our meal is ready."

It looked to William as if the peasants were only too happy to stay well away from "Lady Coldbreath" and her guards. Still, Ottomar ordered Ox to remain outside the hut and make sure no one eavesdropped. If the junior Hospitaler resented always being assigned this duty and left out of his companions' deliberations, no one could have told it from his expression. As usual, he seemed happy to do whatever Ottomar told him to do.

The interior of the wattle hut was all one room that nonetheless felt cramped when the travelers crowded in. It smelled of smoke and cooking, held some inexpertly made furniture, and had rushes strewn on the earthen floor.

Thus, it was little different than the peasant's huts on William's father's land back in Devon, homes he'd often visited and in which he'd occasionally spent the night, and he found it unremarkable. Ottomar, however, gave the place a dissatisfied look before settling on a bench.

Meanwhile, Pierangelo regarded his fellow officer with similar displeasure. "Why did you say we were staying the night?" the Templar asked.

"Can you see to travel by night?" Ottomar replied. "Remember, we're well off the route Kolinda used before. Besides, we six have been awake since yesterday morning. We have to sleep sometime, so why not here, indoors, in a place where we can require our hosts to feed us again in the morning?"

Instead of answering, Pierangelo turned to William and Gaspard. "I didn't see any horses. Did you?"

William felt chagrinned that, once they reached the village proper, he hadn't remembered to look.

Gaspard said, "No. I spotted a cart, but I believe it's an oxcart." He turned to Kolinda. "What was that business with the two freakish boys?"

She narrowed her eyes and mustered her thoughts before answering. "Wise men say the Stain runs deep. It's in the water, the earth, everything, and as a result, sometimes unnatural plants grow, and unnatural animals are born. Unnatural people, too, perhaps, and when they're of humble birth and have...talents, the lords of this place draft them into their service. Apparently there's a little ceremony for handing them over, and we just happened to arrive about the time the villagers were expecting to perform it."

Jibril was on his knees before an open chest rummaging through the stooped man's winter clothing and other belongings. Looking around, he asked, "What are these boys' talents?"

Kolinda shook her head. "A true sorceress might be able to look at them and tell, but I can't."

"But you can tell the villagers are afraid of them," Gaspard said. "When the big one knocked down the mother carrying the infant, no one said a word."

"That *could* have just been because they enjoy some sort of privileged status," Ottomar said, "or because the ceremony was underway…but no. No family member shed a tear at the prospect of us marching them away, and when Kolinda explained that's not why we're here, the elder tried to convince her to take them anyway. Timidly, but still. He was more eager to be rid of the freaks than he was concerned about annoying us."

"We could rid the village of them," Pierangelo said.

"Not without revealing we aren't what we're pretending to be," Ottomar said. "Let's just get through the night and continue on our way."

7

S upper featured chicken, or at least it did for the guests. Wandering restlessly around the village afterward, William observed that the inhabitants appeared to be making do with porridge, turnips, and dark bread.

By the time they finished, night had fallen, and afterward, it didn't take long for the villagers to seek their beds. That wasn't profoundly unusual for people who rose with the sun to tend their crops and livestock and had to chop their own firewood and make their own tallow candles, but William had the impression that on this occasion, there might be more to it. The general feeling in the village was that the way to avoid unwelcome attention from the visitors was to hide in one's hut as soon as possible without appearing disrespectful.

It seemed to William that if the peasants believed the strangers were a witch and men-at-arms in service to their lords and were accordingly intimidated, those impostors had little to fear. Still, in a rare moment of accord, Pierangelo and Ottomar agreed that someone should keep watch outside their shelter throughout the night, and this time, the entirety of sentry duty didn't fall to Ox. The younger Hospitaler, Jibril, Gaspard, and William would each take a turn.

So far, William's watch was passing without incident. He spent most of it perched on a stool he'd hauled outside the doorway, but rose periodically and walked around the hut to help keep himself awake and warm and to catch any foes who were creeping up on the back side of the elder's home to…well, do whatever enemies might do in that position.

On one such circuit, he stopped to study the night sky. Surely, despite what Gaspard had said, he could pick out familiar constellations if he tried hard enough. He just had to work out the trick of it.

He couldn't work it out, though, and in fact, the more he peered, the more the half-moon itself looked different than it should have, a hair too large and a shade off the proper color. People called the moon that shined over England and Outremer silver, but that was just a poetic way of saying it was white. The moon in this sky actually did have a hint of argent tinge to it.

William shivered in his gray cloak, and not because of the evening chill. Except in bad dreams, he'd never felt so lost and confused. He liked Kolinda. Witchcraft or no, abduction or no, Pierangelo's condemnation or no, his instinct was to trust her. But he was also aware that he didn't actually know where she was taking them or what any of this meant.

It's a grand adventure, he told himself, *what you've wanted since you were small and what you left England hoping to find.* Perhaps that only meant he was a fool, but holding tight to the idea made him feel a little better.

He returned to his seat and tried to imagine what it would be like if a true war between good and evil were underway, and for some reason everything hinged on his valor. In the middle of his imaginings, a small figure emerged from the dark. Though William wasn't certain, the newcomer's eyes seemed to shine ever so slightly, as a cat's eyes reflecting firelight might.

William reminded himself that, disfigured or not, the person approaching was only a child; he reminded himself too that the soldiers of Lady Sweetbreath—whoever she was —likely dealt with more unsettling things on a regular basis. So he mustn't seem nervous. Instead, he'd be bored and blasé.

The boy planted himself before him, close enough for William to make out the wizened, sagging old man's features. "I want to come with you," he said.

William wished he could ignore that, given that it had already been addressed. But he felt obliged to say something. "Where's the…" His magically granted knowledge of this country's language failed to reveal the correct term for children bearing the Stain…"uh, the other one?"

The deformed boy spat. "Yerzy's asleep. *He'd* be just as happy to stay here forever and lord it over the village. But I want to fight battles and live in Lady Sweetbreath's castle!"

"You'll get your chance," William said, "in just a few more days."

"I want to start now!" said the boy. "In the morning!"

"No," William said. The child glowered as if no one had ever denied him before. Perhaps no one had. "And you'd better mind your tone. Here in this village, you're special. In Lady Sweetbreath's hall, you'll be just another green apprentice with everything to learn and to prove."

He *hoped* that what he'd just said corresponded at least somewhat to the child's understanding of what went on in Lady Sweetbreath's household. The boy presumably knew something about it just from growing up hereabouts, whereas William knew nothing. He wished he'd asked Kolinda, but this strange place raised so many questions that it was well nigh impossible to address them all.

To his relief, the boy lowered his eyes and erased the

scowl from his face, although there was still a sullenness about him. "If you knew what I can do," he muttered.

"Lady Coldbreath does know," William said. "She can see it inside you, and I gather she wasn't greatly impressed. Now go away and get to bed."

"I don't sleep," said the wizened child.

"Then find someone else to pester."

"Everybody else is asleep. Tell me what it's like to serve Lady Sweetbreath." He jabbed a finger at the red cross on William's surcoat, visible through the gap between the wings of his cloak. "What does that mean?"

William wished the child had wandered up when Gaspard was standing watch. His fellow Templar was quick-witted enough to concoct lies on the fly and have them ring true. William feared he wouldn't do as well, but since the man he was pretending to be would have no reason for reticence, there was nothing for it but to try.

"It's just the device of my particular company. Red to signify we spill a lot of blood."

The boy grinned. "Me too! I mean, as much as I've been able. I can do a lot more!"

"You'll get your chance. Now take yourself off—"

"Tell me about your armor."

William had no idea what the boy was getting at. "What about it?"

"It's different than what the lady's warriors usually wear. The ones who come here, I mean."

That was precious little help. Did they not have mail in these lands?

William extended his arm to give the boy a look at the sleeve of his hauberk. "You have a keen eye. This is different. The smiths have only just started making them. For those of us who are always in the forefront of the fighting. The links stop a sword stroke very well."

The child nodded. "You were at Fire Hill, then. You and your friends. You must have been!"

Inwardly, William winced. He'd hoped a little embellishment would make him sound more convincing, but it had led the boy to draw an inference it might be risky to contradict. Guessing Fire Hill had been a battle, he said, "We saw some of it. I confess, on that occasion, others saw more. We had to march a long way and were late arriving."

"Did you kill any Flinters?"

"One. It truly is late, and all this chatter is apt to wake—"

"I can keep my voice down. What magic did Lady Sweetbreath cast?"

William had felt on treacherous ground spinning lies about heraldry, armor, and a battle he knew nothing about, but lying about sorcery could only be worse. What powers did Lady Sweetbreath command? God's bones, what powers did *any* witch command except the power to drag poor souls hundreds of leagues in an instant and thrust them into problems that were none of their affair?

"She split open the ground and called devils out of Hell to fight alongside us." It seemed like the sort of thing a sorceress might do.

The boy's ever-so-faintly luminous eyes narrowed in a way that, just for an instant, gave his freakishly old face a resemblance to Kolinda's youthful one. "How many?" he asked.

"I'm not sure. I could only see my own part of the battlefield. But…maybe a dozen?"

The boy grunted. "I wish I could have seen it. Thank you for telling me. I'll leave you alone now."

A moment ago, William had feared his peculiar interrogator was going to bombard him with dozens of questions. Now, suddenly, the boy was ready to depart, and even though that was what he'd hoped for, the reality didn't ease his anxiety. It heightened it.

"You don't have to go," he said. "I was starting to enjoy the company."

But the boy was already turning away, and the words didn't pull him back around. He trotted off into the night, and the Templar watched him disappear.

William briefly deliberated. Then he went into the hut, knelt beside Gaspard, and took hold of his shoulder.

Gaspard came awake instantly, lifted the naked dagger in his hand, and lowered it again when he discerned who'd woken him. "What?" he whispered.

"Something's wrong," William said, "or it may be. I can't be certain."

"Wake everyone. Quietly."

They did. Afterward the red light of the dying coals in the fire pit just sufficed for William to tell one of his companions from another.

"Tell us," Pierangelo growled.

William swallowed. "One of the two boys—the one with the old man's face—came and talked to me. He asked me questions about this Lady Sweetbreath and what it was like to be one of her men-at-arms, and I made up things as best I could. But I'm afraid I said something wrong, something he knew couldn't be true, and roused his suspicions."

"Why do you think that?" Gaspard asked.

"One moment, he seemed eager to talk the night away. The next, he scurried off."

"And you just let him go?" Pierangelo said. "You should have stopped him!"

"Not necessarily," Ottomar said. "We don't *know* Sir William said anything suspicious. Perhaps the boy simply had a change of mood. We can't know how such an imp's mind works." He looked to Kolinda. "Unless you do."

The priestess shook her head. "No."

Gaspard picked up his hauberk from the bench where he'd set it down. The mail clinked. "We should go now. It won't be easy traveling through unfamiliar country at night, but we can grope our way in the right general direction."

"Are we sure it's necessary?" Ottomar said. "We don't know for certain the child is suspicious. Even if he is, we don't know that he can persuade anyone else to credit or act on his suspicions. The rest of the village hates him, after all. But if we seven sneak off in the middle of the night, that will absolutely reveal that we weren't who we claimed to be, whereupon the peasants are likely to send word to their masters."

"I understand what you're saying," Gaspard replied, "but can we afford to gamble that the child suspects nothing, or that nothing unfortunate will happen as a result of his suspicions? There could be a runner racing toward the nearest garrison of Sweetbreath's soldiers even as we speak. Our hosts could be arming themselves this very moment."

Ottomar sighed. "You're right. We should prepare to move out."

Pierangelo looked to William. "You're already prepared. Resume your watch."

,William stepped back outside. As far as he could tell, the village was quiet. So far. He considered drawing his sword but didn't because *that* might rouse some observer's suspicions even if nothing had before.

Jibril was the next to emerge, because, William surmised, he hadn't needed to pull on a coat of mail in tight quarters and thus had been able to prepare more quickly than the knights fumbling around and getting in one another's way in the darkness of the hut.

The Saracen was munching on a hunk of dark bread left-over from supper. He tore off a piece and offered it to William.

William was too tense to feel like eating. But Gaspard would tell him to eat anyway because he didn't know how soon the chance would come again. He took the morsel and thanked the Saracen.

Jibril chewed, swallowed, and brushed a crumb or two out of his beard. "Don't blame yourself. You were pretending to be a sort of person you know nothing about. That would have been difficult even for a trained deceiver."

"But I could have done something to the boy, just as Sir Pierangelo said. Instead I let him walk away."

"Soldiers can slaughter defenseless women and children when a commander has given the order, and all their comrades are obeying it. But striking down one little boy— even an abomination cursed by the djinn—on your own initiative, simply because he *might* be suspicious, is a different matter." Jibril sighed. "It may speak well of you that you didn't do it."

William wasn't sure how to answer. The rest of the travelers came out of the hut and saved him the necessity.

"Let's go," Ottomar whispered.

Gaspard pointed. "That way?" he asked, also keeping his voice low. "It's the shortest way out of the village. After we're clear, we can swing west."

"Yes," Pierangelo said, and then a dozen shadows emerged from their hiding places behind other huts, the two deformed boys in the lead and the men of the village, now armed with the axes they used to chop wood, pitchforks, boar spears, and a couple longbows, behind. The child with the wizened face *had* mustered his fellows. He'd just been so stealthy about it that William hadn't detected any sign of it until this moment.

The boy sneered. "Running away." The phosphorescent

eyes were still dim, but now the foxfire glow was unmistakable.

Kolinda stepped forward. Her scowl conveyed haughtiness once more. "No, idiot child. My divinations revealed where the trespassers we're hunting have camped for the night. We mean to catch them while they're sleeping."

The wizened boy laughed, a high, harsh sound like a donkey braying. "Funny. That's how *I* wanted to catch *you*. But maybe this is better. It will impress Lady Sweetbreath even more."

"What are you babbling about?" Kolinda asked.

"Your man there said the lady called up a dozen devils to fight the Flinters at Fire Hill. But everybody knows the Father of Vipers wouldn't take sides in that fight. She had to use other magic."

William had only a vague notion of what all that meant. He suspected Kolinda didn't understand, either, but she kept her mask of arrogance in place. "You don't know anything," she said, and then shifted her gaze to the stooped village elder, who was currently clutching a sledge. "Are you going to let this child's nonsense lead you into a fight you can't possibly win? I'm coven-daughter to your mistress. My guards are trained warriors. We'll butcher you one and all, then put this miserable collection of stys to the torch!"

The elder opened his mouth, then appeared to realize he didn't know how to answer. Like the other village men, he was hanging back and seemed to have little stomach for a confrontation. He simply hadn't felt able to refuse the wizened boy's demands.

But if he was hesitant, the child wasn't. "All right, *coven-daughter*," he said, "let's see your magic. I'll show you mine." He folded his arms and lowered his gaze, his posture and expression bespeaking concentration. No longer squeamish about attacking a little boy, William wished he had a bow, arbalest, or javelin to strike across the intervening distance.

Yet nothing happened. After a few moments, it occurred to William that the boy might not possess magical abilities after all. He might just be a freakish unfortunate everyone had mistaken for a child touched by the Stain, whatever that truly was. The thought nearly tickled a laugh of relief out of him, and then Gaspard breathed, "God's nails."

William looked where his fellow Templar was looking. During the brief time when the boy with the old man's face had held everyone's attention on him, his fellow, Yerzy, had begun to change.

At first William thought the wizened child *did* have magic but not the ability to aim it, because it looked like something was ripping Yerzy to bits in a welter of flying blood and flayed skin. Then he perceived that the force destroying the outside of the child's body was being exerted from the inside. That oversized toddler's form was like a cocoon, and now the moth wanted out. Perhaps it would have come forth eventually anyway, but the witch boy's power was evoking it.

Impossibly, the Yerzy who tore his way free was bigger than the body that had contained him. He stood half again as tall as the tallest man there, and patches and strips of some-thing dark studded his now-naked torso—he'd torn out of his clothing as well as his skin—and ran along his limbs. His arms had stretched long and appeared to have too many joints or joints in the wrong places while the hands had enlarged into huge knobby things even as they shed the little finger. Yerzy's legs, however, remained short in relation to the rest of him. He roared, clenched his hands into fists like the heads of maces, and waddled forward.

"Templars!" Pierangelo snapped. "With me! The rest of you, deal with the witch boy and the villagers." He drew his sword and advanced to meet Yerzy.

Gaspard and William followed, even though William didn't want to. Now that he faced this monstrosity, dreams of knightly glory had lost their appeal. But duty and loyalty made it impossible to do otherwise.

"Surround it," Gaspard murmured. William assumed the words were meant primarily for him even though his friend had his gaze fixed on the ogre-ish thing before them. "Attack when it isn't looking at you, and get away when it pivots to face you. I'll wager it isn't nimble on those stumpy legs."

Pierangelo planted himself right in front of Yerzy. The thing that had been a boy moments before swung his fist in a potentially bone-shattering horizontal arc. The senior Templar ducked below the blow, straightened up, and cut quickly enough to strike Yerzy's forearm while it was still in reach. The creature roared again, perhaps just in rage, although William hoped it was pain.

Meanwhile, he and Gaspard maneuvered behind Yerzy. William cut at the creature's spine, but his blade grated on two of the dark strips and glanced harmlessly away. The strips were some sort of hard shell armoring the flesh beneath.

An arrow streaked past William, then Yerzy lurched around to strike at him. He scrambled backward as Gaspard had instructed and poised himself to duck or dodge as Pierangelo had. But he couldn't retreat far enough quickly enough, and when the backhand blow leapt at him, he wasn't fast enough to twist out of the way. The attack caught him in the torso, smashed the wind out of him, and hurled him off his feet.

With fists raised for follow-up blows, Yerzy took a lumbering step after him, and William knew he should spring to his feet and defend himself but couldn't manage it. Perhaps he'd taken some ghastly wound that severed the connection between will and limbs.

Bellowing, Gaspard and Pierangelo struck furiously at their hulking adversary and, after an instant, distracted him. With a roar, Yerzy turned and struck down at Gaspard, who leapt back out of the way. The creature's fist bashed a dent in the ground and sent dirt flying.

William gasped in a breath and tried again to rise. This time, floundering, he rolled off his back and onto his knees. Maybe he wasn't crippled or grievously wounded after all. Maybe his attempts at evasion had kept Yerzy's blow from striking him as solidly as it might have, and his hauberk had protected him from some of the impact.

Turning over provided a glimpse of the rest of the battle. The wizened boy had retreated behind the village men who were, perhaps reluctantly, servicing as his protectors and once again stood in his stance of concentration. Evidently, he was trying to summon the power for another evil miracle.

Ottomar, Ox, Jibril, and even Kolinda were striving to reach him before he succeeded but hadn't broken through the line of villagers. The villagers had the advantage of numbers and the prudence to fight defensively.

At least the Hospitalers and the Saracen didn't appear to be in any immediate danger from the peasants with their axes and scythes. Kolinda, however, did. She'd brought a mace and a long fighting knife on her journey east, but judging from the awkward, tentative way she was handling them, no one had ever trained her in their use. Jabbing with a boar spear, a towheaded peasant looked as if he might be on the verge of penetrating her guard, and, judging from her wide-eyed expression of desperation, she realized it. But her expression changed to one of cold resolve. The farmer thrust the spear at her face, and she swung the mace in a circular parry. It was still a clumsy move, but it sufficed to sweep the attack out of line and immobilize the spear, and before her opponent could pull it back and free it, she lunged and stabbed the knife into his stomach.

William took all of that in in an instant, and then, finishing the task of heaving himself to his feet, turned away from them. He had his own task to perform in the battle, the task his superior had assigned him.

Yerzy now had bloody slashes between the protective strips of shell. Pierangelo and Gaspard had aimed their strokes to land where the armor wasn't and, at least some of the time, scored despite the added difficulty. But Yerzy hadn't slowed down. He was assailing the Templars as savagely as before, and when Pierangelo cut at him, he grabbed the knight's sword by the blade, jerked it away, and, heedless of the gashes he was inflicting on his own hands and the new blood that flowed from them, snapped the weapon in two and threw the pieces to the ground.

Gaspard drove in at Yerzy, and, shouting and slashing, distracted the child of the Stain from Pierangelo in his moment of unarmed vulnerability. The senior knight fell back and, for want of anything better, drew his dagger from its sheath.

William suspected neither of his fellow Templars could last more than a moment or two longer if he didn't help them. He rushed at Yerzy from behind.

Yerzy didn't seem to sense him coming and didn't even try to turn around. William was able to take an instant to aim, plant his feet to exert every iota of his strength, and cut deep into the small of his back.

The Stained boy screamed and staggered. William thought he might have delivered a killing blow until Yerzy whirled in his direction.

At once, Gaspard sprang in and cut low, at the back of Yerzy's knee. The brute's pivot became a helpless topple, and he thudded to the ground.

Gaspard and William came at Yerzy from two sides and cut repeatedly at spine, neck, and head. Yerzy tried to lift himself up, but failed. After three more sword strokes, he stopped moving altogether.

Panting, the two Templars regarded one another over the top of the corpse. Gaspard gave William a nod, drew a long breath, took a fresh grip on his sword hilt, and turned toward the rest of the battle. William turned as well, and then the night broke into flickering chaos.

The darkness became absolute, then flared into brightness that dazzled rather than revealed. William's mother scolded, "Don't—" before her voice gave way to the cawing of crows. His mouth filled with a taste of venison that changed to sourness, his nostrils caught in turn the smells of smoke and a coming storm, and the heft of a shield weighed his left arm.

After a moment, the phantom sensations vanished, and the night became as it had been before. Except that now his sword, dark and wet down the length of its blade with Yerzy's blood, was the most fascinating thing he'd ever seen. Suddenly unconcerned with winning the remainder of the battle, he stared at it, transfixed.

Though he no longer cared about his companions or their foes, he nonetheless discerned some of them in a murky sort of way beyond the blade that was the focus of his attention. His allies had faltered as he had. The village men could have dispatched them while they stood staring at their weapons, but they held back, possibly afraid to interfere in something uncanny.

After a few moments, William's fascination began to alter. At first the sword had simply been the most captivating thing anyone could ever encounter. He could have stood and gazed at it for days. But gradually that passive contemplation gave way to something else. It was no longer enough to look at the sword. He wanted to bring the edge to the artery on the side of his neck, saw at it, and feel the blade bite.

Except no. *Want* was the wrong word. Slashing his neck would kill him, and he wanted to live. But he somehow *needed* to do it despite the inevitable result.

Fear of death woke his understanding, and he realized that the wizened boy had succeeded in working a second piece of magic. The brief disordering of his senses had been the witchcraft forcing its way into his mind, and the compulsion that now gripped him was the intended effect.

Unfortunately, comprehension didn't break its hold on him. Though he strained against it, a bit at a time, he was bringing the sword into position to harm himself. By the looks of it, his companions were doing the same.

He told himself they weren't all in his field of vision, and surely one of the ones he couldn't see was faring better. Pierangelo's faith and fervor would enable him to break free, or Kolinda's own magic would allow her to resist. She had, after all, cast spells even if she denied she was a genuine witch.

But if either the Templar leader or the priestess was capable of defying the boy with the old man's face, there was as yet no sign of it, and time was running out. Hand shaking with the clash of warning urges, William slid the end of his sword inside his mail coif to lie against bare skin and the pulse that hammered underneath. Tears brimmed in his eyes.

Then the boy sorcerer laughed his whinnying laugh, and although William remained incapable of moving the sword away from his neck, though the pressure to commit suicide was still irresistible, the compulsion wasn't compelling the lethal slice quite yet. Its forbearance reminded him of a cat playing with a captured mouse.

Two or three of the surviving village men cried out. Others stumbled. Then they too stared at their weapons, and in time, resisting as impotently as their foes had resisted, started to poise them to take their own lives.

The wrinkled boy had said he relished killing. Drunk on this great exercise of his power, he'd apparently decided to slaughter everyone in view, the fugitives and the village men who resented him alike.

One by one, the farmers brought their axes, sickles, and arrows into position. William guessed that once everyone had, all the wizened boy's puppets would cut or stab simultaneously in a single climactic moment of self-destruction. He kept struggling to slide the sword out of his mail coif but to no avail.

Ox gave a strangled cry and jerked his sword away from his throat. He lumbered forward as though he was still shedding the last vestige of the witch boy's subversion of his will.

Retreating, the child of the Stain stared at the oncoming Hospitaler in what seemed an attempt to reassert control. It didn't stop Ox's advance.

Some of the village men swayed and stumbled a step, and they all turned their weapons away from themselves, as the wizened boy released his hold on them. "Kill him!" he screamed. "Kill him, and I won't hurt you!" But after what he'd done to them already, his cry failed to spur them into action.

The wizened boy spun around and ran. Ox ran faster and cut him down from behind.

8

W hen the witch child dropped, William's paralysis fell away. His fellow Templars, Ottomar, Jibril, and Kolinda relaxed as well.

Smiling a wolfish smile, Pierangelo advanced on the farmers. Losing his sword might have placed him at a considerable disadvantage when fighting a horror like Yerzy, but he clearly thought a knight in mail wielding a dagger was well up to the task of killing peasants.

Spreading out to encircle the foe, William, Gaspard, Ottomar, and Jibril followed his lead. The villagers fell back before them. Some turned to flee, but, standing over the corpse of the witch boy, Ox was already behind them, cutting off their retreat.

The stooped village elder threw his bow and the arrow he was holding to the ground. Some of his fellows disarmed themselves in the same fashion. "We surrender!" he cried.

"That's sensible," Pierangelo said. "We'll make this fast and painless."

"No!" Kolinda said. "They yielded! You can't just butcher them!"

"We only fought because Ezak told us to!" the elder said. William inferred Ezak had been the name of the wizened boy.

"You fought," said Jibril. "It doesn't matter why." He looked at Kolinda. "Are these not the very Easterners against whom you wish us to wage war?"

The priestess hesitated. "I summoned you to fight the sorcerer lords, their creatures, and their armies."

"I think," Jibril said, his tone gentle, "that you've never actually seen war. If you had, you'd know that when yours starts, it will kill a great many people besides those fighting in the armies, including folk more innocent than these. Why, then, should the slaughter not begin here?"

"Because it's unnecessary," Kolinda said.

"But it's not," Ottomar said. "We know that soon, enemy soldiers will come here expecting to collect Yerzy and Ezak. Imagine their ire if they find out the freaks are dead, and the peasants didn't even send word that we came here and killed the horrible things on our way through. Obviously, they *must* send word at their earliest opportunity...if we give them the chance."

"We'll lie!" said the stooped man. "We'll say the boys died in an accident!"

"Both of them?" Gaspard asked.

"We'll think of *something!*" the elder said.

"I doubt it," Ottomar said. "Not when the truth would serve you better."

"Think about it," Kolinda said. "To ensure silence, we'd have to kill everyone, the women and children, too!"

The senior Hospitaler's expression was somber but resolute. "I have thought about it."

"Why are we still standing here prattling?" Pierangelo asked. "The decision has been made." He resumed his advance, and the peasants scrambled to recover the weapons they'd dropped before.

"Stop!" Kolinda cried. "I forbid it!"

Pierangelo looked back at her. "*You* forbid it."

She took a breath. "I know you don't think of me as the leader or even trust me. At times you speak and act as if I'm your prisoner. But how would you manage without my guidance?"

"What becomes of your great plan," Gaspard replied, "if you deny us your help, and we never reach these Western lands of yours?"

"I don't know," the priestess said. "I'm praying it doesn't come to that."

"It needn't," Ottomar said. "We can compel your cooperation."

"Possibly," Gaspard said, "but we'd lose time we can't afford doing it." He turned to the stooped man. "You're going to send word of us to your masters. As Sir Ottomar said, it's in your best interest, so don't bother denying it. But can you hold off for a little while? Perhaps Yerzy and Ezak went into the forest today and didn't come out again. You searched for them and eventually found the bodies, but not until tomorrow around midday."

The elder said, "I promise!"

Gaspard turned to Pierangelo. "If we move out now, that gives us a good head start."

"Assuming we can believe the promise," Ottomar grumbled.

Pierangelo didn't look any happier than the senior Hospitaler sounded. But he glared at the village men and said, "Leave your weapons where they lie. Bring us food, a way to carry it, and a water bottle for every man. You," he said as he jabbed his dagger at the elder, "stay and tell us about the countryside hereabouts. Everyone else, *move!*"

The other peasants scurried to obey him. Pierangelo strode up and looked over the weapons they'd left behind on the ground.

William wiped the blood from his sword on the tunic of one of the two village men who hadn't survived the battle, moved up beside Pierangelo, and proffered the blade hilt first. "Sir."

"What's this?" Pierangelo asked.

"It...it doesn't seem right that the knight who is my captain should lack for a sword."

The older Templar grunted. "It's yours, and though you were a pitiful excuse for a sentry, you fought reasonably well with it. Keep it. I'll make do." He picked up an axe and gave it an experimental swing.

That one didn't satisfy him, but another did. Meanwhile, William found himself a longbow and a quiver of arrows. A bow wasn't a particularly knightly weapon, but it could prove useful in battle and for hunting as well. He might as well carry it until he procured a shield.

Pierangelo, Ottomar, and Kolinda questioned the elder, the villagers brought provisions in knapsacks, and then the travelers headed out. Periodically, William glanced over his shoulder. He was reasonably certain no one from the village would shadow them. The farmers were too cowed. But he wondered if he might glimpse a runner departing immediately to inform on him and his companions.

Gaspard noticed and gave him a crooked grin. "Wondering if the villagers will keep their promise?"

"Yes," William said.

"That's one of the annoying things about war. You never know as much as you'd like to. You just have to glean what you can, make a decision, and see how things fall out. You'll get used to the uncertainty."

But where would that happen, William wondered, *here or in*

Outremer? The evidence was accumulating that the lords of the Stained Lands were as wicked, as in need of opposing, as Kolinda claimed. The parchment men and the cyclopean dog-thing had been abominations, and by virtue of their humanity, ruined as it was, Yerzy and Ezak had been worse. Yet it was plain that Pierangelo still mistrusted Kolinda as a sorceress herself, believed that when pagan fought pagan, there was nothing to choose, and held that in any case, the Crusaders' duty lay elsewhere.

William supposed that if there was no way home, there was no need to choose, and should a way materialize, well, it still wasn't his place to decide. It was his task to follow where his commander led.

As he reflected on the situation, the fugitives trekked on, sometimes skirting more fields and pastures, sometimes hiking deeper into scrub and wooded areas. Despite all that the travelers had recently endured, the three Templars were clearly one little group keeping more or less together. The two Hospitalers and Jibril formed another group, and Kolinda walked by herself. Her threat back in the village had deepened the divide between her and the men she'd whisked away from Acre, and plainly, she felt it.

Eventually, though, as everyone was seeking a way around a thicket, and an owl hooted at them from a branch overhead, Gaspard left his fellow Templars to walk beside her. William felt a touch of guilt that he kept eavesdropping on his companions, but in this place where he constantly felt bewildered, it was difficult to pass up any chance to learn anything. Trying not to be obvious about it, he eased close enough to Gaspard and Kolinda to have a fair chance of overhearing whatever they might choose to say.

At first, there was nothing. Kolinda simply gave Gaspard a look that seemed to ask his intentions. He replied with a nod that, William supposed, might have conveyed in some subtle fashion that he hadn't come to berate her. They walked on together for a time.

Eventually Gaspard murmured, "That was a good ruse, saying you wouldn't guide us anymore."

"What makes you think it was a ruse?" she replied.

"It wasn't?"

Kolinda hesitated. "I don't truly know. It doesn't matter now, does it? I wanted you all to give me my way, and you did."

Gaspard chuckled. "We did at that. You should know, though, that if you keep pushing Sir Pierangelo, he'll eventually push back as a matter of pride, the consequences be damned. Nor would I wish to get on Sir Ottomar's bad side. My sense of him is that he'll keep smiling but start looking for the right moment to plant his dagger in your back."

Kolinda frowned. "You don't like them."

"I didn't say that. They're hard men, each in his way, but so am I."

"Ready to kill helpless farmers on command?"

"It wouldn't have been the pleasantest duty I've ever performed, but yes."

"Yet you helped find another way."

"When neither side seemed willing to relent, somebody had to suggest a compromise. Mind the spider web." He pointed to the strands that were all but invisible in the night, and they swung around it.

After several more paces, she said, "I'm not a fool."

"I didn't think you were."

"Despite what Jibril said, I know what war is. I mean, I've never experienced it, but I have *some* understanding of it. I know that Easterners who are more or less blameless for the offenses of their masters might have to suffer. I *didn't* know how it would feel to kill one myself."

"It was in self-defense."

"But I still feel sick and ashamed. Except for the Stained creatures, only two villagers died, and *I* killed one of them. At first I didn't think I had it in me, and I was sure he was going to kill me instead, but then something came over me."

"And after the peasants surrendered, the prospect of further killing was intolerable."

"I suppose."

"Well, it all worked out, give or take, and with luck, we won't need to fight again before we get where we're going."

Though it seemed to take some effort, she managed a smile. "Meanwhile, you champions proved yourselves. Proved I did right to draw you out of your world and into this one."

Gaspard gave her a wry look as though *now* he suspected she was a fool. "How do you figure?"

"You destroyed parchment men and killed two creatures of the Stain."

"We only bested the paper men because there happened to be a pool of water handy, and William stumbled on the trick of it. We were only able to deal with Yerzy and Ezak because Ezak was stupid and didn't finish us off as soon as he had us in his power. In other words, our successes were mostly luck, even though the parchment men, terrible as they seemed to us, were really just mindless instruments, and Yerzy and Ezak were only children untrained in the use of their abilities. How, then, do you expect us to hold our own against the Stain's more formidable agents?"

"Somehow, you'll find a way," Kolinda said. "You have to."

With that, they fell silent again, perhaps because Gaspard deemed it pointless to keep arguing that he and his fellows truly weren't the invincible heroes of her imaginings. She'd seen plenty of evidence already, and if she chose to discount it, what more was there to say? Or possibly it had occurred to him that if by persuading her, he might also convince her she had no reason to further concern herself with their welfare.

Because he'd drawn an early watch back in the village, William had had even less rest than most of his companions. His eyelids drooped, and his feet grew clumsy as he trudged along, skirting more pastureland. Periodically he gave his head a quick shake in an effort to stay alert.

In time, the farmland on their right ran up against a wall of trees. The forest before them smelled swampy, and for a moment, William thought he heard a faint liquid sound.

Kolinda had looked like she too was succumbing to somnolence for the last little while, but now she roused. "Was that the river I heard?" she asked.

"I don't know," Gaspard said, "was it? You're the one who'd know."

"I didn't think we'd come far enough west," she said. "But perhaps the map I studied didn't show the river's course perfectly, and the elder's description of the countryside was vague beyond the village's own fields and woodland."

Pierangelo made a disgusted spitting noise at her uncertainty. "Whether the river is near or far, the plan remains the same, doesn't it? To march west?"

"Yes," Kolinda said.

"Then let's go."

They skulked forward, and the night grew even darker as the branches overhead blocked out the moon and starlight. The boggy smell grew stronger, and their feet sank into mucky earth. The sucking sound when they pulled them free masked the liquid sounds farther off when the latter recurred.

Reluctant to ask a question of the company at large lest he provoke another scornful response from Pierangelo, William moved closer to Gaspard and Kolinda and said, "Am I hearing the river again?"

Gaspard smiled. "You're hearing *something*, but I doubt it's that. The sound of a river flowing wouldn't be so intermittent. Nor, now that we've entered this patch of woods, would it be coming from behind us as well as ahead."

William felt a pang of alarm. "Is it?"

"I believe so, but I have no idea what it means." He turned his head toward Kolinda. "Do you?"

"No," she said.

"Should we warn the others?" William asked.

"I considered it," Gaspard said, "but warn them of what? It's not the sound of people or even animals sneaking around. Should we stop for another argument about something that may well be harmless? I'd rather press on and get clear of it. Just stay alert."

William found he had no difficulty doing as the older Templar had bade him. The revelation that the faint noise was coming from *every* direction, that something might have *surrounded* them or be *stalking* them, was more than sufficient to open his eyes wide and banish sleepiness. Yet when trouble came, it caught him by surprise.

As a rule, no one in the company was better at creeping along quietly and avoiding obstacles and difficult ground than Jibril. Even so, he took a step, and his leg plunged into the soft earth halfway up to the knee. He gave a little snarl of vexation as he strained to pull it free, and Ox chuckled in a good-natured way to see his predicament.

Covered in mud, Jibril's leg started to come out, then plunged again, almost as if someone more powerful were yanking the mired end of it. At the same moment, his other foot sank in above the ankle.

Still grinning as though his companion's plight was more amusing than anything, Ox stepped forward and held out his hand.

"Don't!' Ottomar cried.

Ox stopped and looked around at him in perplexity. Meanwhile, Jibril sank deeper, both legs mired nearly up to the hips.

"It's quicksand," the senior Hospitaler said. "Go closer, and you risk sinking yourself. We need something that will bridge the distance and that we can use to drag him out."

William wondered if it was quicksand or something else. It had certainly looked like something *jerked* Jibril's leg down into the ground, but perhaps that wasn't really so.

In any case, whatever was actually happening, Ottomar probably had indicated the safest way of extricating Jibril. William looked around for a fallen branch that was long and sturdy enough. He couldn't find one.

Apparently no one else could, either, and after a moment, Ox reached up, gripped the low-hanging branch of an oak, and, with a teeth-baring growl of effort, pulled. Wood snapped, and then the branch came down in a rattle of twigs and leaves.

Gaspard hurried to him to help him manage the limb more deftly, they extended it, and Jibril gripped an end section that looked heavy enough to bear the strain of his weight and the quicksand's clinging resistance. A bit at a time, Jibril's legs began to lurch forth from their imprisonment. William strode to help his fellow knights pull, and then Kolinda gasped.

Startled, William peered this way and that to see what had alarmed her. For a moment, in the darkness, he couldn't tell. Then he looked down and could just make out the small ripples running through the ground. The waves were converging on the patch of earth on which she stood as though the ground were a pond and someone had *un*thrown a stone into it. With them came the fluid sound he'd caught before, the sound, he now realized, of mud sliding on mud.

Some forming into crude facsimiles of arms and hands,

lengths of muck rose beside Jibril's upper body and wrapped around or clutched at him. At the same time, other such extrusions took hold of the broken branch. The trapped man lurched back breastbone-deep into the ground. The tree limb lurched, too, as the mud sought to wrest it from the knights' hands. Gaspard did lose his grip, but, with another snarl of effort, Ox jerked the branch up and loose. Dirt showered down from the piece of wood as the lengths of muck that had been clutching it stretched beyond their limits and fell apart.

With three men pulling, William told himself, they'd haul Jibril free despite the worst the mud could do. Then he felt the ground further softening under his own boots. Except that it wasn't *only* softening. It was *squirming*, and the shock of it balked him even before Pierangelo shouted, "Get away!"

William looked at his captain in confusion.

"He's a Saracen," Pierangelo said, backing toward firmer ground. "We'd pull him out if it were safe, but it's not."

"Damn you!" Ottomar said. Though he too was retreating.

Kolinda wasn't. She was scurrying to grasp the tree limb. Meanwhile, Ox and Gaspard's feet sank into the earth until they were mostly covered. The dirt around them humped and rippled with the threat of grasping extrusions to come.

A comrade, albeit a Saracen, was in danger. Christian knights, including William's friend, had imperiled themselves to save him, and now a woman was doing the same. William couldn't just turn away, despite Pierangelo's order. He too ran as best he was able on the sucking, treacherous ground to seize hold of the branch.

Yet even after he gripped it, he and his companions were at best keeping the mud from pulling Jibril in any deeper. They weren't pulling him free, and even the stalemate wasn't going to last as they too were being drawn down, just more slowly. They repeatedly had to stop straining at the task at hand to extricate feet that would otherwise have been trapped in the muck.

William felt a length of mud coiling and crawling up his leg like a serpent. With a gasp of loathing, he yanked his limb free and stamped the extrusion into clods and spatters.

At his back, Pierangelo said, "We can't lose everyone! But if I'm risking the mud, so are you!" A moment later, both he and Ottomar took hold of the limb.

It still wasn't enough. Even the six of them straining together couldn't pull Jibril out. For much of its length, the branch was now covered in mud as tendrils and malformed hands of muck sought to wrest it away.

The ground under William's feet grew softer still. Kolinda cried out as both her legs plunged in almost up to the knee. Gaspard had to let go of the branch momentarily to help her free herself, and Jibril sank a couple inches deeper.

"Leave me!" the Saracen said.

"Do *not* let go of the branch!" Gaspard snarled back. "Not until we do!"

"What?" Kolinda said.

"We're going to pull our hardest while I count to three," Gaspard replied. "*On* three, we're all going to let go at once, and Ox and I are going to rush to Jibril and try to pull him out with our hands. The rest of you will follow, get behind us, pull on us, and anchor us. Clear?"

Ox grunted. "I can do that."

"You don't know this will work," Ottomar said.

"We'll find out," Gaspard said. "One...two...*three!*"

They all let go simultaneously, and Gaspard led them in a scramble that swung wide before looping in toward Jibril. At the same time, Jibril sank in almost up to his neck.

Yet it wasn't as deep as William had expected. Apparently the mire had diverted some of its strength from pulling on

Jibril's lower body to pull on the oak branch, and when it abruptly took sole possession of the length of wood, it didn't adjust instantly. If it possessed anything resembling a human mind, perhaps it was confused.

The travelers' semicircular path avoided much of the softest earth. It also ended with them behind Jibril when they'd been in front of him before. Maybe that would confuse the mud, too.

Gaspard grabbed one of Jibril's hands, and Ox, the other. William caught hold of Gaspard's sword belt and felt someone doing the same for him.

Some grunting with the effort, they all pulled. Jibril gasped as if something about the dragging or the muck's counter-pulling pained him. He slid free a few inches but then plunged down again. The ground softened under William's feet as the mud redirected its strength.

"Again!" Pierangelo shouted. "With everything you have!"

William tried his best, presumably everyone else did, too, and then, covered in mud, the extrusions gripping his shoulders and forearms falling apart, Jibril slid free. His rescuers staggered and floundered, recovered their balance, and Ottomar said, "Run! Back the way we came!"

They did flee, and the malevolence in the ground did its best to catch them. Ripples of mud made the fluid sound William had heard before, and periodically the earth softened under his pounding feet. But nobody dropped into it as Jibril had. The power could lie in wait and catch prey by stealth but seemed unable to gather itself in one spot quickly enough to chase a running person down.

When the fugitives drew even with the farmland again, the signs of pursuit ceased. William guessed they'd crossed some sort of boundary. They staggered to a stop, and then, glaring at Gaspard, Pierangelo panted, "You disobeyed my order!"

Gaspard blinked in confusion, or at least put on the appearance of it. "Did I, sir? Then I beg forgiveness. In all the confusion, I didn't hear."

Pierangelo rounded on William. "I know you heard."

"I did, sir," the youngest Templar said, "but Gaspard, one of our brothers, was in trouble, and then a woman, and…and you said yourself that if Satan puts a demon squarely in our path, we should fight it."

"A demon," Pierangelo said, "not mud." Still, he now seemed willing to let the matter drop.

But not everyone was. Staring at Pierangelo, Jibril said, "*I* heard the order you gave as well."

Pierangelo stared back. "And you saw me help save you, idol worshiper though you are. Be satisfied with that."

"'Idol worshiper?'" Jibril replied, half outraged, half incredulous. "How can you have lived side by side with us for so long and know nothing?"

"I know you don't follow our Lord Jesus Christ. It's all I need to know."

"Please," Ottomar said, "lay this quarrel to rest, or at least suspend it for the time being. We have urgent matters to discuss." He turned to Kolinda. "Was the evil in the ground a spell cast by one of your Eastern witches to hinder us? Have they located us? Are their forces closing in?" He looked around. "I don't detect any signs of it."

Kolinda's eyes narrowed as she pondered. "Perhaps we're all right. There's a phenomenon I've heard rumors about. People say the Stain itself can run wild in a particular patch of ground, and when it does, strange things happen there. It's only supposed to happen farther east, where Nature's wounds are deeper, but if people have started casting dark magic and mustering corrupted troops closer to the river, perhaps it could happen here as well."

Gaspard smiled. "No matter why it happened, it's nice to

think that enemy soldiers aren't about to emerge from the darkness. I'd at least like to catch my breath prior to any more excitement. How much ground has the Stain poisoned? Can we detour around it?"

"You understand, until tonight, I didn't even know for certain that this really happens. I'm still not completely sure that what we encountered was the Stain running amok of its own volition. But if it was, it may well have contaminated that whole forest."

"Which stands as a barrier before us," Ottomar said. "We'll have to go either south or north to get around it."

"We came from the south," Gaspard said, "well, southeast to be precise, but anyway, the south is presumably where the wardens of Anjalor's old temple are still hunting us."

"But to the north," Kolinda said, "the land is more densely populated. There's a town, Meerjhaj, and the farms and hamlets that keep it fed."

"Well," Gaspard said, "perhaps our pursuers will think we're not stupid enough to go farther north and accordingly won't look there. We'll also make better time on roads than pushing through the woods. I think we should try it."

Ottomar nodded thoughtfully, and Pierangelo said, "Agreed."

9

The first road was nothing more than a narrow, overgrown path with old wheel ruts and animal droppings on it. After a while, though, it merged with another, the two combining to make a slightly broader, better defined way than either of its tributaries. The process repeated itself as the wayfarers hiked north.

As the morning advanced, they made their way past farmland more often than not, and, trudging wearily, William was struck again by a general impression of blight. The crops looked stunted and were sometimes spotted with the brown slime he'd noticed previously.

One field was crawling with little black locusts with yellow heads. A hundred crows cawed, wheeled above the rows, and swooped down from overhead, but even their rapacity wasn't likely to check the insects' gluttony before they spoiled the crop. There were just too many locusts. In a pasture, two sheep lay dead and stinking with bloody froth on their mouths. Their wool had fallen out in patches, and the flesh beneath looked rotten with gangrene.

When it was plain that fatigue was wearing on everyone,

even the stolid Ox, the travelers took refuge in a copse of elms they hoped would hide them from passersby on the road. Apparently it did, for, sooner than William would have liked, Pierangelo was nudging him with the toe of his boot, not exactly kicking but not too far short of it either, to wake him because it was time to move on.

Their route turned, angling them toward the afternoon sun, and William tugged on the hood of his cloak in an effort to shade his eyes against the glare. Then their way came to a broader one, a true highway at last, though he'd never seen one quite like it. It was paved with stone and humped up slightly in the middle, perhaps to facilitate drainage into the ditches that, like footpaths and bridleways, ran along either side.

"Interesting," Gaspard said.

Kolinda peered at him. "What is? It's just a road."

"A better one, I think, than those that run through our lands."

"I've seen what's left of old Roman roads," Ottomar said. "I can imagine they looked like this in their day."

Pierangelo made a spitting sound. "Do you Hospitalers make a study of pagan things? It wouldn't surprise me. Let's go." He tramped off down the nearer footpath, perhaps because of a feeling they'd all be less conspicuous there than marching down the middle of the primary thoroughfare.

His companions followed, and William wondered anew what six men-at-arms from Acre could possibly do to justify Kolinda's faith in them. Her people commanded sorcery, and now it seemed they were also better at mundane tasks like building roads. He didn't *want* to believe the priestess was a fool and her beloved prophecy the delusion of a lunatic, but common sense inclined to that conclusion and suggested Pierangelo had the right idea. The sooner they found a way home, the better.

But then again, common sense would have denied that Joshua could knock down the walls of Jericho by blowing trumpets or that Samson could kill a thousand Philistines with the jawbone of a donkey, but everyone knew that with God's help, those things had happened. Perhaps, then, something of the sort could happen in the present day, and if so, where better than here, where wonders and miracles abounded, even if all the ones he'd encountered so far were the work of Hell.

The road climbed to the top of a rise, and then the travelers saw that its continuation ran through a settlement at the bottom of the slope on the other side. Except that it wasn't just a settlement anymore. Rows of red and yellow tents stood beside the wooden buildings, banners fluttered in the fitful breeze, and people were everywhere. The figures were too tiny with distance to tell a great deal about them, but occasionally the afternoon sun glinted on what was surely armor. A kind of muddled drone rose from the scene, and a rhythmic clanging indicated that somewhere amid the swarm, a smith was at his labors.

Pierangelo said what must have been apparent to them all. "An army has taken that town for a base of operations."

"Is this Meerjhaj?" Ottomar asked.

Shading her eyes, Kolinda peered. "I don't believe so. I don't see the river on the far side of it. I think it's the first town east of Meerjhaj."

"What's its name?" the senior Hospitaler asked.

"I don't know."

Pierangelo scowled. "How helpful."

"I told you," she said, "I wasn't expecting we'd come this way."

"Whatever it's called," Gaspard said, "do we go around or through?"

"Through," Jibril said. "There are surely pickets and

patrols beyond the borders of the town, and if they spot us sneaking through the countryside, we'll have no hope of persuading them we are innocent travelers. Whereas if Lady Coldbreath and her retainers walk calmly through the camp, no one will think anything about it."

Kolinda frowned. "I was game to impersonate one of Sweetbreath's deputies when we were just trying to fool a few peasants. But this—"

"Should be no more difficult," Jibril said. "How do you think spies manage to infiltrate fortresses and the courts of kings? It's *because* there are so many people that no one knows everybody else, and numbers and guards make everyone feel safe."

Kolinda looked unconvinced.

"I'd pretend to be leader and act as spokesman myself," Jibril continued, "except that I wouldn't be credible in the role unless I obtained a change of clothes." Though he'd made an effort to clean them, his garments were still filthy with dried mud. "If you truly don't feel up to it, perhaps Ottomar, Pierangelo, or even Gaspard—"

"No," William said. Everyone turned to regard him, he felt a flash of embarrassment, and pressed on anyway. "As far as this place is concerned, there's something funny about our mail. Well, maybe. Ezak thought there was, and if there is, it might be better not to draw attention to it."

"Is that true?" Gaspard spread his cloak to give Kolinda a better look at the hauberk beneath.

"I think so," she said. "Perhaps. I don't know a great deal about armor."

"But you do know these lands better than any of us," Gaspard said. "That's why you should speak for us in any case. I know you're up to the challenge."

She took a deep breath. "All right. Surely we haven't come this far only to meet with disaster now."

"We need to move," Pierangelo said. "We've already stood here chattering too long. Someone looking up the road could have noticed our hesitation."

They set off for the town, and Kolinda wrapped herself in the arrogant demeanor that had fooled the villagers. A sentry came to meet her at the stone archway that William supposed was technically the town "gate" even though the place wasn't walled.

The sentry was a stocky man whose drooping mustache ends bracketed a mouth full of green-stained teeth. Perhaps the color came from something he'd recently eaten or ate habitually. His armor was indeed not mail, but rather fashioned of iron strips held together with straps to protect his chest and shoulders, and his round helmet was made of bronze with a neck guard. He had an oval shield, too, but had left it leaning against one side of the arch near where his partner was loitering. For an instant, William had the thought that he might be able to filch the shield as he passed and be properly equipped at last, and then he recognized that only an idiot would try.

Indeed, he wasn't sure the soldier would let them into town at all. Now that it was too late to turn back, it struck him that Kolinda might be striding along like a person of importance, but her clothing wasn't fancy, nor were the nondescript cloaks of her companions. Though only Jibril was filthy from toe to neck, after their ordeal with the living mud, everyone was dirty, and Pierangelo was carrying a woodcutter's axe instead of a proper weapon. Moreover, everybody was on foot, and in all likelihood, coven-daughters traveled on horseback or in conveyances whenever conditions permitted it.

The sentry's casual approach, and the fact that his comrade wasn't bothering, drove home the fact that people hereabouts weren't as easily impressed as the villagers had been. "Your names and your business," he said.

"I'm Coldbreath," Kolinda said, "coven-daughter to Lady Sweetbreath, and these are my retainers."

The sentry stood up straighter but frowned as well. "We were told Lady Coldbreath was coming, but..." He seemed doubtful Kolinda was who she claimed to be yet also reluctant to risk offending the real Coldbreath by saying so outright.

"An accident on the road," Kolinda said with the hauteur of one who disliked explaining her circumstances to an inferior. "Some of my people stayed behind to rescue the baggage and sort out the mess. Now stand aside."

The sentry hesitated. "Of course, my lady. Or better still, allow me to send for someone who can escort you directly to the houses Lady Sweetbreath has taken for herself and her followers. The camp can be a maze if you don't know your way around."

Kolinda made a show of inhaling deeply, then slowly blew the air in the sentry's face.

The warrior blanched. "My lady? What—"

"Wait a moment. You'll feel it. It's how I answer disrespect."

Judging from the sweat that broke out on the soldier's brow, maybe he truly did feel something, or rather, imagined he did. "My lady, please. If I showed disrespect—"

"You *delayed* me," Kolinda said. "You suggested my powers are so paltry they can't guide me to my coven-mother's quarters."

"I beg forgiveness! Truly, I didn't mean any of that!"

Kolinda blew more air into the sentry's face, this time quickly, as if she were puffing out a candle. "The spell's gone. Now get out of the way."

The sentry did so with alacrity, and the fugitives marched

on into the bustle of the town subsumed by a military camp. In the intersection of two streets, more warriors were drilling with spears. A man pushing a wheelbarrow approached and looked over the spot, then, evidently deciding there was no room to pass through without risking life and limb, grimaced and went back the way he'd come.

Jibril came up to walk near Kolinda. "You handled that nicely," he murmured.

"I agree," Ottomar said, "although now we're in the same hive of the enemy as Sweetbreath, with the real Coldbreath herself due to arrive at any moment."

"I couldn't know Sweetbreath was here," Kolinda said. "I didn't even know there was a real Coldbreath. I simply made up what I thought was a likely name."

Gaspard grinned. "If we ever get shields again, I propose painting 'I didn't know' on them as our new motto. Truly, priestess, our friends are right. You did well. Now we just have to make our way to the other end of town and take our leave with reasonable haste, before anything happens to unmask us."

They walked on. William did his best to look like he belonged and to hide any signs of jumpiness, and after a time, he started to relax. As best he could judge, no one was paying any particular attention to him and his companions. Moreover, while he was younger and less experienced than any of his fellow knights, he'd been one long enough to feel at home in military camps, and really, this was just another such.

Well, not entirely. Occasionally, at a distance, he caught a glimpse of the magic and the unnatural beasts the sorcerer lords commanded. He saw a tubby, balding man in a red cassock smeared colors—predominantly puke-yellow and magenta—in the empty air as if he were finger-painting on a wall. When the ugly oval was complete, everything nearby stretched and strained toward it like water seeking a drain until he swiped a clear slash across his creation an instant later. Vultures with wings made of fire harried a trainer's assistant who wore a mask and heavy, baggy clothing that evidently protected him against beaks, talons, and combustion. Still, William thought that as long as he didn't turn a corner and come face to face with something profoundly unnerving, he'd be able to hide the combination of dread and curiosity such sights inspired.

His luck held until he and the others reached the far end of the town. There was another pair of sentries guarding the road running out of the settlement to the west, and these two had a One-Eyed Hound with them. Though currently just lying on its belly with a horse trough full of water and a mostly devoured pig carcass nearby, the enormous six-legged beast was no less alarming in the daylight.

William took a breath and told himself that for the moment, the creature wasn't hostile. It looked like it would be happy to take its ease in the sunlight unless its masters commanded it into action, which meant Kolinda simply had to practice her deception as she had before.

She gave the sentries a cool nod as she and her companions neared the arch. Unfortunately, her air of prideful self-assurance didn't stop both guards from placing themselves in her path. The taller of the two, a man of about Pierangelo's age with deep-set brown eyes under scraggly brows, said, "I need to see your passes."

Kolinda scowled. "Does no one in this camp recognize a coven-daughter of Lady Sweetbreath?"

The guard put on an expression that managed to be more respectful but resolute at the same time. "My lady, I beg your pardon. But our orders are that *no one* goes west of here without a pass. If you like, I can send Lynath here to verify that everything's in order. There's a tavern right across the way where you can wait in comfort."

"That won't be necessary," Kolinda said. "I'll sort this out myself." She wheeled and led her companions away from the arch.

When they were far enough away that the guards wouldn't overhear, Pierangelo said, "Why didn't you do the blowing trick?"

"Because my sense of this sentry was that it wouldn't work on him," Kolinda replied, "and then he'd know without a doubt that I was an impostor."

Ox slid his fingers inside his mail coil and scratched an itch. "Why won't they let us go farther west?"

"They don't want Westerners boating on the river or looking from the far bank to see their troops mustering," Gaspard replied, "so they're keeping most of them back until they're ready to cross over."

"Exactly," Pierangelo said. "How do we move onward? It would be God's work to kill the demon dog."

"But the whole rest of the camp would fall on us while we were trying," Gaspard said. "I share your sentiments, sir, but I think that once again, we need to sneak. We don't have to exit the hamlet via the highway. We can slip out at another point and pick up the road farther along."

"After nightfall," Jibril said. "Our chances will be better."

They found a narrow little cul-de-sac in which to wait, a spot removed from most of the bustle of the camp where they hoped to be inconspicuous. William felt as though the sun was sinking with excruciating slowness. Footsore and tired as he still was, he tried to make the most of this opportunity to rest, but worry interfered.

What if a guard at either the eastern or western arch decided the exchange with "Lady Coldbreath" had been peculiar enough to warrant discussing the matter with a superior? What if, despite the fugitives' attempt to remove themselves from view, someone spotted them and remarked on their unfamiliar armor, the strange emblems on their surcoats, or some other anomaly? What if the hunters from the old temple arrived in town and told everyone they were on the trail of a woman and six men? What if, what if, what if?

He regarded Ox with a certain envy. The Hospitaler was slumped and snoring.

A bit later, evidently recognizing William's anxiety, Pierangelo gave him a sour look. "If you can't sleep," the senior Templar said, "pray."

William did so silently to avoid disturbing his fellows or being overheard by a villager or Stained Lands soldier. Even though the horrible thought came to him that he might be so far removed from Christendom that the Lord Himself couldn't hear him.

Perhaps prayer helped settle his mind despite that blasphemous notion. For suddenly it was dark, he too was slumped against a wall, and Pierangelo was once again nudging him awake with the toe of his boot.

"It's time," said the older knight.

A path ran between houses on the western edge of the settlement. Jibril had taken it upon himself to scout it, and now he emerged from the darkness.

"Everyone seems to be asleep," the Saracen whispered, "and I don't think there are any dogs. Beyond the houses are trees. If there are guards, they're not making noise or showing light I can detect from here."

"In short," Gaspard said, "this is as likely a way out of the village as we're apt to find."

"Let's move," Pierangelo said. "Quietly."

The gloom grew thicker with every step the fugitives took away from the lamps and campfires burning in the town at their backs. The homes to either side were just vague lumps in the gloom, but nearer to the path, William could make out chicken coops to the right and a pigpen to the left. The fowl and the pig were presumably asleep, but noise could wake them. He resolved to creep along even more carefully.

Suddenly, off to the left, something yowled. Startled, he

pivoted in that direction, and his hauberk clinked. He winced at the noise.

"Cat," Gaspard whispered. "Let's get clear before someone comes to a window to throw something at it."

Now still skulking but also trying to move more quickly, the travelers advanced while the cat screeched on and on behind them. The path grew indistinct, and the trees, black pillars in the night, loomed before them. Then, as Gaspard had predicted, a man cursed, presumably threw something, and the cat yowled a different, affronted sort of yowl. William grinned because he was confident he and his companions had crept far enough past that the fellow wouldn't spot them.

Beneath the trees, the night was dark enough that he couldn't tell what kind of trees they were until his foot bumped something, he peered down to see what, and found an apple. The wood was an orchard, which, he belatedly realized, explained why there were straight, easily negotiable lanes between the rows of trees.

It was, he thought, a stroke of luck, or perhaps the answer to the prayers he'd prayed back in the cul-de-sac even if he had dozed off on God in the middle of them. Evidently deciding to make the most of the easy going and put the sorcerer lords' encampment far behind them, Pierangelo quickened his stride, and his companions quickened theirs to keep pace with him.

For a time, their progress was uneventful. Then Jibril whispered, "Stop!"

A moment later, William understood why. Presumably cast by a bull's eye lantern, a ray of light was playing about among the trees ahead.

The fugitives scrambled for cover. Hiding behind a tree trunk, William told himself that the beam of light hadn't fallen on any of them. If they were sufficiently stealthy, then the person ahead, whoever it was, might wander on his way without detecting them.

Then something huge came snuffling forward, with an odd rhythm to its gait that came from having more legs than four. It was another One-Eyed Hound, and its low rumble of a growl confirmed that, with the breeze blowing at William's back, *this* beast absolutely *had* taken the travelers' scent.

Apparently Gaspard had concluded the same. He stepped into plain view, William followed his lead, and others did the same.

"Good evening, friends," Gaspard said.

"Who's there?" replied the man with the lantern. Though staying behind the One-Eyed Hound, he and his partner were coming forward, too. As the second man advanced through a spot where moonlight fell on him, the additional illumination revealed the shape of armor.

"Your fellow soldiers," Gaspard said. "We just wanted some apples."

The guard barked a truncated laugh. "Then the joke's on you. They're either green or shriveled, and now you'll have to answer to the sergeants."

Gaspard spread his hands. "Surely there's no need for that. Haven't you ever disobeyed an order when it wouldn't hurt anything?"

"Not one that came down from Lord Stonebreaker himself."

"Maybe there are no good, ripe apples, but we have wine. We'll share."

"Maybe the sergeant will give us the jug as a reward. Turn around and march back the way you came."

William wondered if his fellow Templar hadn't tried to pass Kolinda off as Lady Coldbreath because he deemed it unbelievable that such a personage would be wandering around an orchard to pick her own apples in the dead of night. Mostly, though, his mouth dry, the younger knight wondered what was going to happen next.

The One-Eyed Hound was just a few paces away when the answer came. A shadow appeared behind the soldier with the lantern. The soldier made a choking sound and collapsed. His partner pivoted, but before he could level his spear, the shadow rushed him and slashed. The second warrior fell with blood spurting from his neck, and William saw the curve of the sword that delivered the lethal cuts.

He realized that not all of his companions had revealed themselves when Gaspard did. While the others held the Stained Lands soldiers' attention, Jibril had sneaked around behind the two men on patrol with such consummate stealth that even the One-Eyed Hound hadn't noticed him moving. Then he'd killed them.

That left the gigantic animal still alive, but it hadn't received a command to attack and, William suspected, might not bear its masters any great affection. It swung around toward the carnage and let out another growl but didn't lunge at Jibril. Yet.

In another moment, though, it likely would. The smell of spilled blood and the realization its masters were no longer capable of restraining it would energize such a monstrous beast with the lust to kill.

Pierangelo ran forward with his axe upraised and chopped at one of the Hound's hind legs. The beast snarled and spun back around. The Templar captain sprang backward just in time to avoid a bite that would otherwise have torn off his head. Fangs like swords clashed shut an arm's length from his face.

Meanwhile, the other fugitives charged the Hound. Gaspard yelled in an apparent effort to distract the brute from the vulnerable man right in front of its jaws, and William did the same.

The shouting didn't work. The Hound lunged and snapped a second time. Pierangelo dodged the gnashing jaws, but the creature's foreleg bumped him and knocked him on his back. Lowering its head, the beast then lunged again.

Before it could snap up Pierangelo, though, Gaspard and William closed with it and assailed it from two sides. William tried to cut the glaring Cyclops eye, but the Hound snatched its head high while he was swinging his sword, and he merely inflicted a shallow gash on the dewlap instead.

Pierangelo scrambled to his feet, and the other fugitives caught up to him and his fellow Templars. They all spread out to surround and attack the One-Eyed Hound, even Kolinda awkwardly flailing with her mace.

William hoped seven-to-one odds, even if the seven were little, puny things compared to the one, might convince the latter to break away. They didn't. Vicious as he'd imagined it to be, the One-Eyed Hound showed no inclination to retreat. It meant to kill the humans no matter what wounds and pain it endured in the process, and over the course of the next few moments, he grew increasingly fearful it would succeed in doing precisely that.

Even close up, in the gloom the Hound's dark, thick hide combined with its startling quickness made it difficult to score more than superficial slashes. William cut at the beast's legs—they were the most accessible targets, and if he and his comrades crippled enough of them, the unnatural animal would fall wallowing and vulnerable on the ground. William's sword connected with the beast's legs sometimes, but never with the sort of tendon-severing or bone-breaking stroke he needed.

As he tried and failed to maim it, the Hound whirled back and forth to attack one target and then another. Given its size and weight, its unpredictable pivoting was scarcely less dangerous than its bite. It made William feel like a fly avoiding the swings of whatever implement some human being was employing in an attempt to swat it. Until he didn't avoid one.

Someone cried out. It might have been a cry of distress. William cast about to see if a comrade was in trouble, and at that same instant the One-Eyed Hound turned, and a middle leg slammed into him and knocked him sprawling. The limb took another rapid step, and he rolled out from underneath to keep the paw at the end from squashing him.

The frantic evasion put him farther away from the creature, and as he sucked in a breath and drew himself to his feet, he had a better view of the battle as a whole. *Someone* had succeeded in inflicting significant damage on a leg. The Hound was holding one forepaw off the ground, but, with five functional limbs remaining, was spinning and lunging as agilely as before. The creature whirled toward Kolinda, and she jumped back, but its strike still tore the mace from her hand to be gnashed to pieces and then swallowed. She fumbled her knife from its sheath.

William peered for another moment in an effort to determine if the outcry he'd heard meant one of his comrades was disabled or worse. As best he could tell in the murk and confusion, none of them was lying on the ground. But Gaspard abruptly turned and ran away from the Hound.

The younger Templar was shocked. Of everyone he'd met since arriving in Outremer, Gaspard was the man he'd liked and trusted most. Still, he supposed this unequal struggle with a horror out of Hell could break anyone's nerve. But it wasn't going to break his! He raised his sword and advanced on the One-Eyed Hound again.

It turned and, in so doing, presented him with its hindquarters. It was arguably the safest position from which to attack, and, heartened, he rushed in hoping to cripple a hind leg. Before he could close the distance, though, the

Hound spun once more, its jaws gaped and reached, slaver flew from them, and then a gust of the beast's hot, fetid breath stung William's eyes and face.

William dodged, and the bite missed. But before he could come back on the offensive, the One-Eyed Hound tried again, and then kept coming. Some of his companions were surely slashing at it, but their efforts failed to distract it. Perhaps, in its wolfish or demonic mind, it had decided that the way to win the battle was to orient on one foe, pursue him relentlessly until he was dead, and then move on to the next.

William took one retreat and then another. There was no time to glance back and see where he was going, only to defend and defend and look for an opening that would allow him to strike back to good effect.

That opening never came, but Gaspard dashed out of the darkness and stabbed a short length of wood into the Hound's flank. "Down!" he shouted as if he were commanding an ordinary dog. "Down!"

William realized his friend hadn't fled the battle after all. Recalling that one of the warriors back at the ancient temple had referred to controlling and disciplining his Hound with a "rod," he'd run to the bodies of the men Jibril had just killed in search of such an implement. He'd found one, too, or believed he had, and was now attempting to put it to use.

Unfortunately, to no avail. Still chasing William, the Hound gave no sign it even noticed the prodding or the shouting that accompanied it. Had he breath to spare, the younger knight would have urged Gaspard to cast away the worthless stick and resume attacking with the sword he currently held in his off hand.

Instead, the other Templar darted away again.

Moments later, William's back foot came down on something that rolled beneath it and sent him reeling. An apple, he thought, as he floundered backward. A low-hanging branch caught his flailing arm, jerked him partway around, and he fell on his side. Certain he wouldn't be fast enough, he sought to flop over onto his back and lift his blade to pierce the jaws that were surely hurtling at him even now.

But enormous fangs didn't close on his mail and the flesh beneath with rending, crushing force, nor did he feel the jolt of the sword piercing some part of the Hound's anatomy. Rather, the beast let out another ear-splitting howl and, thrashing and rolling, nearly tumbled over Ox as he scrambled backward.

Gaspard had given the rod to Kolinda, and now she was jabbing the Hound with it.

"Quickly!" Gaspard called. "While it's hurting!"

William's fellow men-at-arms rushed in cutting. He scrambled up and did the same.

The hound's writhing could still pulverize someone who wasn't nimble enough to keep it from rolling on top of him, but even so, when William didn't have to worry about the beast's jaws snapping at him in a purposeful attack, it was easier to score with cuts and to land them where they looked like they might do real damage. He slashed at the one great eye and produced a gush of fluid.

Perhaps in response to that grievous injury, the Hound flinched and rolled beyond Kolinda's reach. She started after the creature, it sprang to its feet, and she recoiled to keep it from trampling her. Nostrils flaring, presumably blind but still not helpless, the beast came at William again.

At the same moment, though, Pierangelo charged and swung the gory axe at the side of the Hound's head. Bone crunched, and the creature's lunge became a helpless sprawling as its still-functional legs buckled beneath it.

Even after the One-Eyed Hound stopped moving, the fugitives kept hacking the carcass for a while until everyone was sure it was dead or simply ran out of breath. Ottomar turned to Gaspard and wheezed, "Well done."

"Thank you, sir," Gaspard replied. "But Kolinda deserves the credit." He smiled. "Well, most of it. She's the one who was able to use the rod."

The priestess looked more puzzled, perhaps even troubled, than pleased at her success. "There should have been a triggering word. Or something comparable. I don't understand *why* it worked for me."

"Because you're a witch," Pierangelo said. "The Devil looks after his own."

Gaspard's mouth tightened in seeming annoyance, but he apparently decided his superior's statement was better ignored than challenged directly. "Obviously, Kolinda, I did give you the rod because of the spells you worked previously. I reasoned you have magic inside of you whether you consider yourself a true sorceress or not, and I was right."

"You reasoned that," she replied, "because you don't know how magic works." She waved the rod to indicate the two human corpses on the ground. "They weren't sorcerers, but they were able to use the rod because they knew the trick. I don't, so..." She shook her head.

Gaspard snorted. "Well, I don't have the knowledge to argue the matter, and really, what does it matter anyway? Just hold on to the rod in case we need it again."

Now it was Pierangelo's turn to scowl as if he would have preferred Kolinda cast an instrument of witchcraft away. But he left *that* opinion unspoken. Perhaps because a weapon was a weapon, and the fugitives might need all they could lay their hands on.

The senior Templar left his axe embedded in the Hound's body, examined the swords the two dead soldiers had never had the chance to use, and took one of them and a spear for himself. The other men-at-arms cleaned their blades,

Ottomar claimed the remaining spear, and William retrieved the bow he'd hastily tossed aside at the start of the melee.

He wished they could all rest for a while, too, but knew there was no time. It was all too likely someone back in the camp had heard the One-Eyed Hound roaring and howling, and even if no one had, the patrol would eventually be missed. When the fugitives moved out, they trotted—their weariness and the weight of their gear be damned.

E ven in the dark, William could tell Meerjhaj was a larger town than the one that now lay behind him and his fellow fugitives. Yet this late at night, it wasn't a similar bustling hive of activity, though yellow light shined through the occasional window and no doubt some people were still on the streets.

"I don't see tents," he said, "or campfires burning. You were right, Gaspard. The Eastern soldiers don't want Westerners to spot them mustering along the river."

"But they still have men in Meerjhaj keeping an eye on things," Gaspard replied. "You can count on it. But with luck, we should be able to make our way to the docks, steal a boat, and cross the river." He looked to Kolinda as though seeking confirmation that that was still the plan.

She nodded. "If we'd been able to keep to the route I intended, we would simply have used the boat I crossed in and left hidden. But since we couldn't, yes, we'll need to take somebody else's."

"Let's do it, then." Pierangelo let his new spear fall from his hand, and scowled at Ottomar when the latter failed to do the same. "The weapon's longer than you are tall, Hospitaler. You can't hide it under your cloak."

Ottomar glowered back, and William wasn't surprised. He was fairly certain that, though the senior Hospitaler had fought competently when it was necessary, in recent years, he'd spent more time at a desk or council table than in the field or training at arms. He was the member of the group showing the most signs of exhaustion and had, off and on, used the spear as a walking staff.

"What about William's bow?" he asked. "Strange that you're only seeking to disarm me."

"He took it from a peasant," Gaspard said, "and unlike that plainly military spear you're holding, it's a weapon anyone might own. If somebody asks, he'll say he's getting home late from hunting."

Ox smiled at Ottomar. "I can help you along if you need it."

"I'm sure that won't be necessary," the senior Hospitaler answered stiffly. With a flick of the forearm that made the action ostentatious, he too dropped his spear. "Shall we?"

The fugitives headed down the hillside from which they'd been surveying the settlement ahead. They'd kept off the road lest pursuers from the encampment to the east come racing up behind them, but they had made reasonably good time nonetheless, hurrying through more cultivated land and open country as opposed to wild forest and Stain-cursed bog.

But because they'd kept clear of the highway, the travelers had no way of knowing if word of their flight had reached Meerjhaj before them. William took what comfort he could from the fact that he could perceive no sign of search parties in the jumble of buildings beyond the bottom of the hill, although really, anything could be waiting in the murky, tangled streets.

Jibril took the lead, an arrangement that even Pierangelo had seemingly come to accept as a matter of course. No one in the group possessed sharper senses or could move more stealthily, and perhaps the Templar captain had decided that even a Saracen wouldn't betray his Christian companions in these circumstances. After all, for whom would he do it, and to what end?

Limping, Ottomar brought up the rear. Ox hovered beside him, ready to take his arm or catch him if he started to fall until the older man waved him away.

They all entered Meerjhaj in much the same fashion that they'd exited the previous town. They advanced along a muddy path that ran between houses on the periphery of the settlement, only this time without a screeching cat to complicate the process.

As they penetrated deeper into the town, and the black bulks of benighted buildings rose on every side, William felt penned in and tried his best to shake it. He should be feeling emboldened with safety nearly in his grasp. For whatever Kolinda's Western kingdoms were, they apparently weren't lands of black magic where existence would be an endless ordeal of running from devil worshipers with actual devils on their trail. He adjusted his hood and cloak in an effort to better hide his sword and mail and walked on. He hoped he and his companions looked like just one more group of nondescript townsfolk traversing the dark streets together.

The travelers sometimes had to backtrack when a street came to an unexpected end or turned in the wrong direction. Still, they were finding their way west, and without attracting any particular notice as far as he could tell. William repeatedly breathed deeply, hoping to smell river water and listened for the creak of mooring ropes and the boats they bound to the docks, until a sustained noise he couldn't quite identify blared through the streets. It might have been the call of a horn or a voice imitating such a note. Whatever it was, it was jarringly loud. Had he not known better, he would have imagined the source was right behind him.

When the blaring ended, Gaspard snarled, "God's nails!"

Ox blinked. "Do you think that had to do with us?"

The question made Gaspard chuckle. "I think that's a good guess." He looked around at all his companions. "Our pursuers are with us again, but they're too late. One last little dash to the river and we're clear. Come on!" He set off running, and his companions did the same. With Ox once more beside him, Ottomar was at the tail end of the procession but more or less keeping up.

Alarmed or made curious by the noise that had just faded away, people in the buildings to either side peered out doors and windows at the men in the street, who, now that they were in headlong flight, had no chance of passing for innocent folk abroad on innocent late-night business. William hoped a mob wouldn't come pouring out of the houses to accost them.

That didn't happen. But people shouted, "They're here!" and "This way!" and "They're heading west!" to help the hunters locate their prey. Keeping pace with them, the clamor surrounded the fugitives like a cloud of angry wasps.

Still, William and his companions rounded a twist in the street and there, at the end of a final length of thoroughfare, was the riverfront. Black in the night, the masts of moored sailboats drew angles on the different darkness of the sky. He couldn't truly see how wide the river was, but from what Kolinda had said, it was wide indeed, a great natural divide between East and West and a barrier to hinder pursuit once he and his comrades cast off from the docks.

They were halfway there when warriors ran into view and formed a double line barring the end of the street.

William reflexively stumbled to a halt, and his companions did, too. The newcomers had them outnumbered at least two to one and presumably weren't exhausted, either.

After a moment, Pierangelo spat, perhaps to show contempt for the foe, perhaps to scorn himself and his fellow fugitives for hesitating. "God wills it," he said, drawing his sword.

"Allahu akbar," Jibril replied. From his tone, he was agreeing with Pierangelo in his own way. He readied his scimitar, the remaining fugitives unsheathed their blades, and they all charged together. The bow slung across William's back bounce-bounce-bounced against his spine, and he wished he'd thought to set it aside as he had before fighting the One-Eyed Hound. But he couldn't stop and fall behind to attend to that now.

Spears jutted from the enemy formation. As he rushed in, William used his sword to knock away one that was poised to impale him, employed his off hand to shove aside another, and then he was in sword range. He cut at a face as young as his own, the spearman's eyes widened in dismay, and then the blade split his countenance in two.

The youthful spearman fell backward. William turned in search of a new opponent and found a man about to spear him in the back. He struck at the spear and loosened his new foe's grip on it, then sprang and slashed while the other man was fumbling. The spearman dropped with blood spurting from his neck. The spray spattered the warrior next to him in the face, and taking advantage of the momentary blinding, Ottomar hacked him down.

Casting about for the next threat, the next adversary he needed to dispose of, William pivoted again and in so doing took in more of the battle as a whole. The charge had broken the double line. Now some Stained Lands soldiers were dropping the spears that were cumbersome at close quarters and were snatching for their swords, while others maneuvered to surround the fugitives and assail them from all sides. Meanwhile, William's companions fought savagely to fell them before the encirclement could happen.

William gasped in a breath and threw himself at one of the swordsmen on the other side. The other man feinted to the head, cut to the chest, and, momentarily deceived, the Templar failed to parry the true attack in time. The enemy warrior's blade gave him a stinging whack across the torso but didn't penetrate his mail. He struck at the wrist of his foe's extended arm, and the warrior dropped his blade and retreated with his hand twitching spastically. Jibril cut him down from behind.

William looked for his next foe. To his surprise, he didn't find one. Somehow, all the sorcerer lords' soldiers were crippled, dead, or running away, and all his companions were still on their feet.

"Keep moving!" Pierangelo said.

They scurried along the docks until Kolinda pointed. "That one!" she gasped.

William knew relatively little about boats, but the choice seemed sound to him, narrow and sharp-prowed enough to cut through the water, small enough for six men to row at a fast clip. No one else voiced any objections, either, and they all piled in, found and readied the oars lying in the bottom of the craft, untied the mooring lines, and pushed off.

As he pulled on his oar, William half expected to see other boats chasing theirs, but he didn't. Though the blaring call had roused Meerjhaj's garrison, the warriors hadn't instantly acted to cover all contingencies, and their disorganization worked to the fugitives' advantage.

Soon, William thought. Soon, he and his companions would be far enough from shore that no enemy boat could catch them even if its crew could pick them out in the darkness. Then, shining as if it were holding and strengthening the moon and starlight, white mist billowed onto the docks. Shrouded by the cloud, only vaguely visible in the midst of it, a shadow walked to the end of the same pier from which the fugitives had cast off. She—William thought from the silhouette that the figure was a woman—knelt down and leaned out over the water. He had decided she must be blowing on it when the first ice appeared beneath her.

Reflecting the sheen of the mist, the ice expanded with unnatural speed, but not in all directions equally. Rather, it ran straight at the fugitives, making a path across the otherwise liquid water as it came.

Gaspard gave Kolinda a crooked smile. "Evidently, when she found out you stole her name, Lady Coldbreath took it personally enough to join the chase."

"I already told you, I didn't know there *was* a real Lady Coldbreath!"

William looked at the western shore. It was still far away, so far that he and his companions had no hope of reaching it before the ice caught up to them. The breadth of the river that had seemed a source of safety only moments before had become part of a trap. It almost felt like the laugh line of a cruel joke.

When he turned back around, William was looking at him. "It's up to you, archer."

"Me?" William asked.

"No one else can hurt her, and if you don't, she's going to freeze the boat in the ice like a fly stuck in a spider web. I don't know exactly what will happen after that, but I'll wager it will be unpleasant."

William swallowed. "All right."

"Stop rowing," Gaspard told the others. "He needs a steady platform to shoot from."

As William picked up the bow from the bottom of the

boat, he noticed there was a little bilge water there. Had the string gotten wet enough to make accuracy impossible? He could only hope not.

He rose, and the boat rocked under him. Even with nobody rowing, Gaspard's attempt to secure "a steady platform" seemed like another mocking joke.

He peered at the distant Coldbreath. Still kneeling, she made a small target, one half concealed by the fog. *Everything* was against him, and this was impossible!

No. No, it couldn't be, because that would mean this was ruin after they'd come so far and that he'd let everyone down. He nocked an arrow, drew it to his ear, and tried to judge how to compensate for exactly how the drifting, bobbing boat was moving.

"Shoot!" Ottomar said. "The ice is nearly here!"

"Quiet," Gaspard said. "Let him concentrate."

William let the arrow fly. The shaft arced through the darkness and buried itself in Coldbreath's body where the shoulder met the neck. She pitched forward, fell off the dock, and landed on the ice she'd created.

The far end of the ice stopped advancing. Ox cheered.

"Now row!" Gaspard said. "Before the whoresons try something else."

As it turned out, the enemy didn't attempt anything else, or at least not quickly enough to prevent the fugitives from reaching the western shore. The bodyguards who rushed out of the thinning fog were too intent on seeing to their fallen mistress to leap into boats and give chase.

But it would still be imprudent for the travelers to linger on the riverbank where searchers would have an easy time finding them. Spent though they were, they hiked away from the river through countryside that, in the dark at least, seemed no different than the land around Meerjhaj.

William noticed they'd fallen into the same little groups

from before, Templars together, the Hospitalers and Jibril the same, and Kolinda walking alone. At moments during the journey west with all its attendant dangers, the seven of them had seemed united, but now the youngest knight had the old familiar sense of grudges, suspicions, and cross-purposes. He fancied he could almost feel the mechanism that was Ottomar's mind working away like a mill or a loom to further his own agenda. Perhaps it was inevitable, but it saddened him.

The travelers found their way to a road. It ran through fields of grain up to a modest keep that, in the darkness, William might almost have mistaken for his father's.

"Thank the Lord." Gaspard grinned at Kolinda. "I assume that as the heroes of Daran's prophecy, we'll receive a lavish welcome."

Kolinda's mouth tightened with what might have been guilt. "There's a lot I haven't told you," she replied.

END OF BOOK ONE

AUTHOR'S NOTE

"Gee, Richard," I imagine you saying, "that didn't seem like the whole story."

Very astute, Hypothetical Reader. Indeed it isn't.

Last year I pitched an epic fantasy series to Jaym Gates, my wise and wonderful editor. She liked the idea and said that Falstaff was really looking for novellas. Could I tell my epic yarn in a series of novellas instead of the usual cinderblock-sized novels?

I could, and the more I considered the suggestion, the more I liked it. So what you just read was the first novella.

I'm eager to continue the saga, but I write for a living as well as the joy of storytelling. That means that the better this novella sells, the sooner I'll get around to cranking out the next one and the ones that follow.

So if you too are eager for me to continue, you might consider recommending this story to your friends and posting reviews on Amazon and elsewhere.

Up to you, of course. Either way, I'm grateful you checked out the story, and I hope you enjoyed it.

ACKNOWLEDGMENTS

Thanks to my editor Jaym Gates and to Robyne Pomroy, Melissa McArthur, John Harness, and everyone at Falstaff Books who helped prepare the book for publication.

ABOUT THE AUTHOR

Richard Lee Byers is the author of over forty fantasy and horror books including *The Things That Crawl, The Hep Cats of Ulthar, This Sword for Hire, Blind God's Bluff, Black Dogs, Black Crowns, Ire of the Void, Undercity, Lancelot, Citadel of Gold,* and the books in the "Impostor" series. He is perhaps best known for his Forgotten Realms novels. One of them, *The Spectral Blaze,* won Diehard GameFAN's award for the Best Game-Based Novel of 2011.

Richard has also published dozens of short stories, scripted a graphic novel (*The Fate of All Fools),* and contributed content to tabletop and electronic games. A film script he wrote based on one of his fantasy novelettes is under option.

Richard lives in the Tampa Bay area and is a frequent guest at Gen Con, Dragon Con, and Florida SF conventions. He invites everyone to Follow him on Twitter (@rleebyers) and Facebook.

FRIENDS OF FALSTAFF

The following people graciously support the work we do at Falstaff Books in bringing you the best of genre fiction's Misfit Toys.

Dino Hicks
Samuel Montgomery-Blinn
Scott Norris
Sheryl R. Hayes
Staci-Leigh Santore

You can join them by signing up as a patron at www.patreon.com/falstaffbooks.

Made in the USA
Middletown, DE
09 September 2020

18772792R00078